Voluptuous

A novella in The Bed Me Books series

Her father's best friend is the man-of-her-dreams.

Lady Henrietta Stafford can't remember a time when she wasn't fascinated by the tall, dark, melancholy Mr. Oliver Hartwell. But she knows she is meant for some other, far less compelling man. Her father's friend would *never* be interested in her. She's too young. She's not beautiful or clever. And, of course, he's already married.

A widower twice over, Oliver Hartwell's life has been marked by failures—his boyhood-dream-turned-hellish-nightmare, his tragic marriages, the utter botch he is making of fatherhood. In truth, he has only ever found happiness in the home of his friend, the Duke of Bexton. But now that his friend's oldest daughter has grown into a gorgeous, voluptuous woman, Oliver seems doomed to ruin his chances for love and affection, just as he has ruined everything else.

In one weak, wicked moment, ruination becomes the first step towards redemption . . .

VOLUPTUOUS

Voluptuous

A Regency romance novella

The Bed Me Books

Felicity Niven

Bletherskite Books

*to women
who deserve love
and haven't found it yet*

really, I write all my books for you

(but well-loved readers are welcome, too)

Contents

Prologue   1

PART ONE
A MARRIAGE OF INCONVENIENCE

Chapter 1   9
Chapter 2   15
Chapter 3   22
Chapter 4   35
Chapter 5   40
Chapter 6   47

PART TWO
A STUDY IN OLIVER

Chapter 7   55
Chapter 8   60
Chapter 9   70
Chapter 10   74
Chapter 11   80
Chapter 12   84
Chapter 13   90

PART THREE
BED ME, HUSBAND

Chapter 14   99
Chapter 15   109
Chapter 16   119
Chapter 17   131
Chapter 18   140
Chapter 19   147

First Epilogue   153

More About Voluptuous	163
Author's Notes	165
Acknowledgments	167
About the Author	169
Also by Felicity Niven	171

PROLOGUE

SEPTEMBER, 1819. CROSSTHWAITE.

"I want a child."

Oliver Hartwell froze behind his newspaper. Everything in his body—his heart, his breath, his mind—came to a halt as the print on the page in front of him swooped and swarmed like a murmuration of starlings.

He forced himself to speak. "You do?"

To his own ears, his voice sounded unnatural, strained, distant.

"Will you give me one?" she asked.

He folded his newspaper with even more care than he usually did. Finally, every page was perfectly aligned, every crease was sharp, and he could not delay any longer. He put the newspaper aside and moved his gaze to the fresh face of his young wife sitting opposite him, her embroidery in her lap.

"You're a girl."

Henrietta had the most womanly body possible, lush and curved and feminine, but she was still so young. Oliver constantly reminded himself of that in an ineffectual bid to keep his thoughts in check.

She blinked, her pale-blue eyes disappearing for a fraction

of a second under her golden lashes. "I am not. I am one-and-twenty."

She was? "And I am forty-three years of age."

She took a deep breath. "Forty-three is not too old. You are capable."

Yes, he was, and she knew it.

Never mind that she had been fully aware he had already sired a son when she married him. Only a week ago, she had caught him in his bedchamber, shamefully hunched over, his cock in one fist and her shift in the other. He had not been able to stop his spend even when he heard her gasp and saw her eyes go wide, her face so white the freckles on her nose stood out in relief, her pink lips forming a shocked *O*.

In fact, her presence had catapulted him over the edge.

Thank God, at least he had not been grunting out her name as he so often did when he yielded to his basest desires. And he prayed she had not recognized her own undergarment in his hand.

Yes, he was more than capable. And with her? His capacity would be endless. He could give her scores of babies, keep her swollen with child for years on end.

"It's not seemly," he said finally.

Her forehead wrinkled in vertical perplexity exactly the way her father's did. "We are husband and wife. What could be more seemly?"

He could not answer that. Because, of course, she was right. Husband and wife were meant to indulge in amorous congress, to be fruitful and multiply.

What was unseemly was their marriage. That a beautiful, vibrant girl full of promise like Henrietta had been consigned to wed a shell of a man because she had a kind heart and he was a weak, selfish fool.

She leaned forward and patted Oliver's hand. A thrill ran through him just as it always did whenever she touched him.

No matter how chaste the contact. No matter that this whole-some, consoling pat was exactly what she would also give his five-year-old son when he scraped his knee.

"The room can be dark," she reassured Oliver. "There would be no need for us to see each other."

Was she modest? She had never struck him as such. She was all exuberant health, not bothered one whit during a game of chase if her skirts hitched up to show a strong ankle, a plump calf. Never bashful when she let herself be caught and she bent over to laugh with Nathaniel and her bodice gaped and showed beads of sweat along the tops of her bountiful breasts, tempting Oliver beyond all reason while he stood under the shade of a tree and watched her gambol with his son.

She sat back. "So, you see, it's all right. The darkness would let us think of another."

She could think of the boy he had kept her from marrying. And he could think of…whom could he think of? For the two years of their marriage, he had thought of no one but her.

Her.

She looked away from him, towards the fire that made the red-gold curls atop her head glint like flames themselves. "And I hope you would tell me how I could please you."

Please him? Was there anything about her that didn't please him?

"Then you understand men derive pleasure from the act of conception," he said carefully.

Her spine straightened, and she turned her head to meet his eyes.

"Yes." A blush spread across her face, and she swallowed. "Did you know women may also derive pleasure from it?"

In principle, yes. But not his wives. Not with him. Not the kind of pleasure he—

Oh.

He'd always assumed Henrietta was a virgin, but perhaps he'd been mistaken. Perhaps her childhood sweetheart had taken her maidenhead before the incident that had forced Oliver and Henrietta together. If so, why hadn't the young man demanded he be the one to wed her? No, the cad had abandoned her, thinking the worst of her, when it had all been perfectly blameless. On her end.

Oliver would like to bash the boy's face for not sparing her from…well, him.

He shifted in his chair. "May I have some time to consider your request?"

"Of course." She smiled politely, but he wasn't deceived. He knew her smiles. She was disappointed.

"I would like to grant your every wish, but—"

"This is sudden," she said quickly. "I have surprised you. And I know I can be rash at times, but this is not a whim. I want to be a mother. I have always wanted to be a mother. I want a baby."

She should want a baby. He believed most women did. And he couldn't imagine any better mother than the one Henrietta would make.

Would make? Come now, he chided himself. There could be no better mother than the one Henrietta already *was*. Because, despite Oliver's cruel insistence Nathaniel not call her Mama, Henrietta was his son's mother in all but blood.

She gave him a real smile now. "And it would be so good for Nathaniel to have siblings. A large family, just like mine. He'll be a splendid big brother."

Something in Oliver's chest reached up and grabbed his throat, choking him, forcing him to blink away tears. He did not deserve to share a house or a name with this miraculous creature who was so unstinting in her love and generosity towards his son.

And she wanted a large family. This would not be a one-

time occurrence. Oliver might be expected—nay, welcome—
in her bed for years to come.

"But I will let you think on it," she said, nodding. "I know
you do nothing without weighing the matter carefully."

Nothing, except importune a girl who only meant to
comfort a sad, old man.

She went on. "And you made it perfectly clear when we
married that we would not— I mean, I know you would
prefer—"

What did she think he would prefer?

"—for us to be as brother and sister."

Never once had he thought of her as a sister.

He had thought of her as someone far too young to be
saddled with him as a husband.

He had thought of her with gratitude and admiration for
how she had gladdened his and Nathaniel's lives and the lives
of everyone around them.

He had thought of her with a deep, dark, pulsing, possessive, disgustingly animal lust.

He had never harbored a single brotherly feeling towards
her.

"Yes, I will think on it."

She beamed at his answer, and he picked up his newspaper
and unfolded it, only to stare at it blindly, completely unable
to comprehend a single sentence.

With just four words—*I want a child*—she had turned his
world topsy-turvy. His orderly mind had dissolved into a
jumble. His usually placid blood raced, a hot and greedy river
drenching every organ of his body.

And dread and hope gnawed at his heart, in equal
measure.

Part One
A Marriage of Inconvenience

ONE

MANY YEARS EARLIER.

Throughout Lady Henrietta Stafford's childhood, Mr. Hartwell visited Bexton Manor many times. He was a friend of her father, the duke, and the two men would sit and drink spirits in her father's study. Perhaps talk and laugh together, too.

Almost certainly, her father would laugh as it was rare that he did not. But, on second thought, maybe Mr. Hartwell wouldn't. Henrietta had never even seen the gentleman smile.

He lived far away in the Lake District, but he often had occasion to travel to London and the duchy of Bexton was a convenient stopping place. His wife—or rather, wives—never came with him.

Mr. Hartwell expressed no curiosity about Henrietta or her brothers and sisters. But she had always been curious about him. So stern, so grave, so silent. So unlike her playful father who had the energy of an unbroken colt. So different from her long-winded mother who couldn't help but speak her mind, especially when it came to her twin passions—Anglo-Saxon runes and her husband.

Sometime between her thirteenth and fourteenth years,

Henrietta would often find herself idling outside the study when Mr. Hartwell came to visit. Hiding her large, tall body was an impossibility, so she didn't even try. She boldly held her head up and stole as many looks at him as she dared when he and her father finally emerged.

His face was all strong planes and sharp angles. His narrow body was all elongated sinew and bone, and he overtopped her very tall and broad father by several inches.

A solitary lock of ebony hair was the one thing that defied the orderliness of Mr. Hartwell's outward form and somberness of dress. When the weather was wet, that lock would spring loose and dangle over his dark brows, a rebellious and naughty curl. She came to love the rainy days that coincided with his visits because she might get a peek at that curl.

And, yes, she found herself thinking of him when she touched herself in her bed at night. Stroking her already-unwieldy and still-growing breasts. Learning her nipples puckered in response to even a light brush of her fingers and a sharp pinch in the same place caused an equally sharp thrill. Allowing her hand to wander over the dome of her belly, down to the place between her thighs where a throb ached under the ginger hair there.

He was married, of course. By the time she had discovered how to bring her private pleasure to a satisfying end, he had a second wife, the first having died. But his marital circumstances made no difference to Henrietta. It wasn't as if she really thought anyone as attractive, as mysterious, as serious as Mr. Hartwell would ever admire someone like her.

Occasionally, she made an earnest effort to turn her nightly thoughts away from him. She would try to think of Lord Ramsey's son. Geoffrey was a nice, simple boy who would become a nice, simple man who would make a good husband for a nice, simple girl like herself.

And her father's title paired with her generous dowry

would make her a good match for Geoffrey. Henrietta didn't really have anything else to offer. She wasn't beautiful like her restless middle sister Ellen or clever like her sharp-tongued youngest sister Amelia.

Still, Geoffrey might choose Henrietta. His parents often hinted at a future union between the two families when they paid neighborly calls at Bexton Manor.

But, despite her best intentions, when her drenched finger brought her to the cusp of ecstasy, Geoffrey's ordinary brown eyes would invariably turn into Mr. Hartwell's smoldering gray ones.

Such a goose she was.

A goose with a honking, hearty laugh just like her father's. She had gotten that from him, along with his red hair and large frame. And like her mother, she had blue eyes, a big bosom, and no secrets.

Well, she had one secret. A *tendre* for the unreachable, unknowable, unbearably desirable Mr. Oliver Hartwell.

The second Mrs. Hartwell died in childbirth the same day Henrietta turned sixteen. When the letter arrived with the news, she couldn't help thinking how sad Mr. Hartwell must be. She knew there was nothing she could do for him herself, but she urged her father to pay a visit.

The duke resisted. "Hartwell wouldn't want to be bothered when he's mourning. Believe me."

Still, she kept after her father, cajoling him to go see his friend. Finally, he had the carriage made ready and took the three-day journey to Crossthwaite, Mr. Hartwell's property near Woldenmere.

Her father returned a fortnight later and came and found her in the stables where she was currying Zephyr.

"You were right, Hen," he said, holding out his hand for

the enormous black gelding to investigate with his muzzle. "The man needed company."

Henrietta straightened up from brushing the silky, white feathering around Zephyr's ankles. "You did him some good?"

He shook his head. "I don't know. I did my best."

She threw her arms around her father's strong neck and bussed his bristly cheek, so grateful he had listened to her and gone to visit Mr. Hartwell. "Thank you, Papa."

Henrietta did not think she should ask for more details of how Mr. Hartwell fared, but she kept her ears open at dinner, knowing her mother would coax something from her father.

"How goes the baby?" her mother asked.

"Poorly. Very weak."

Ask about Mr. Hartwell, Henrietta willed her mother.

"And Oliver himself?" her mother said, right on cue.

"He's—" Her father wiped his mouth. "It's hard to tell. He's a private man."

"But how does he look? Is he drawn? Is he sleeping and eating?"

Her father only shrugged. "He'll weather this. He's weathered worse."

"Hssst," her mother warned her father and cast a meaningful look around the table at the rest of the family.

Worse? What could be worse than having your wife die? Twice now for Mr. Hartwell. Henrietta's heart ached for the poor man. She must think of something she could do from a distance to ease his grief.

The next day, an idea came to her during her morning ride, and when she came back into the house, she went down to the kitchens.

"Mrs. Blaire, would you teach me how to make custard?"

"Custard, my lady? Why would you want to know that?"

In the main, Mr. Hartwell ate very little, but Henrietta had noticed he loved Mrs. Blaire's custard, often finishing two platefuls of it at a single meal. But she couldn't possibly admit her real reason for wanting to learn how to make custard.

"Is it very difficult? Do you think I could manage it?"

Several days of instruction followed with Mrs. Blaire unfailingly producing a perfect custard, while Henrietta's was either a curdy clump or a gritty soup. Mrs. Blaire's custards were not wasted but sent up to grace the dinner table each night. Henrietta's attempts weren't wasted, either; they went to the pigs who would eat anything.

When a flustered, sweaty, covered-in-egg-yolk Henrietta finally produced a gorgeously yellow, thick, silky custard and Mrs. Blaire pronounced it as good as hers, she glowed with a deep satisfaction.

"Now," she said, looking around the kitchen. "What kind of pot should I put it in to send it off?"

Mrs. Blaire frowned. "Send it off? Where, my lady?"

As always, when someone nudged close to Henrietta's secret, she felt herself get hot.

"Oh." The cook nodded knowingly. "To the neighbors. That strapping Ramsey boy. I see."

Until that moment, Henrietta had not remembered Geoffrey also liked Mrs. Blaire's custard and had even been known to pick up his plate and lick it when he was younger.

"What? No, no, no," Henrietta said, horrified. "I want to send it…far away."

"You can't preserve custard and send it off like jam, my lady. It will spoil in a day. How far away did you want to send it?"

"No matter." Henrietta fled the kitchen.

That night, her sister Ellen complained about having custard as a sweet for the fifth night in a row.

"Nothing beats Mrs. Blaire's marvelous custard," her father said and deposited a large spoonful in his mouth.

Henrietta almost blurted out she had been the one to

make this particular custard, but that would almost certainly lead to questions about why she had and she didn't have a ready excuse that didn't include mention of Mr. Hartwell's fondness for custard. Henrietta was a woefully bad liar, and, unlike Mrs. Blaire, her older brother Alexander would needle her until he got the embarrassingly true answer he was after.

So, she kept her mouth shut, only opening her lips to eat the rich custard as her mother began to regale the table with the fact that the word *sweet* came from the Old English *swēte* and the word was likely over five thousand years old.

It was a very good custard.

And it was unjust, Henrietta decided, that a word could last for five thousand years and a very good custard could only last a day.

Two

1817.

The Season after she turned eighteen, Lady Henrietta Stafford was presented at court. As a result, the whole family spent months and months in town with either her mother or father accompanying her to balls. Her brother Alexander refused to act as chaperone, saying he wasn't going to waste time at balls when he hadn't even reached his majority yet. There were far more diverting and far more wicked amusements available in London for a young heir to a duchy.

Yes, young men could wait. Young women weren't supposed to. And some young women didn't want to. Ellen cried and raged and begged to come out as well, even though she was only sixteen.

"It's so unfair! I couldn't possibly be more bored while Hen gets to have all the fun!" she wailed and slammed the bedchamber door in the Bexton town house as Henrietta's lady's maid Lucy struggled to wedge Henrietta's bosom into the cups of her stays before putting her into her ballgown.

It was too bad she couldn't trade places with Ellen. A ball would be the perfect place for her sister's high spirits. And, in truth, Henrietta found balls disagreeable. She would never breathe a word of complaint to anyone, but all of the young lords seemed barely formed and reminded her of her little brother Gideon. None were nearly as interesting or as attractive as Mr. Hartwell.

Or maybe she didn't like balls because she didn't look right? She wasn't always the tallest young lady present, but she was invariably the plumpest.

"I'm too big," she observed to her mother as they stood together and watched the dancing couples.

"No, dear heart, you come from warrior stock on your father's side, and you have generous curves in all the right places, like me, that's all."

It was very good of her mother to call it something else, but Henrietta knew the truth. She was fat. And it appeared fat was not desirable, not fashionable. It was also very good of her mother to take all this time away from her work on the Bexton Codex in order to help Henrietta find a husband.

"You'll have more dances at the next ball," her mother said in the carriage on the way back to the town house in the gray London dawn. Then her face lit up. "After we nap a bit, let's go to the British Museum this afternoon. That's where I met your father, after all. What fun we used to get up to in the manuscript rooms."

"Please, Mama." If Henrietta didn't stop her mother, she'd hear all about the *fun*.

"Such a talented kisser your father was. And still is. And the other things he can do with his—"

"Mama!"

But ardent gentlemen in search of buxom brides did not haunt the British Museum as they had when her mother had been her age. Instead, the place was full of dusty scholars, enchanted to encounter the eccentric Duchess of Bexton and delighted to discuss the finer points of Cædmon's alliterative verse but not the least bit interested in her decidedly dull daughter who didn't know a *hwæt* from a *hwearft*.

Henrietta had to laugh at herself. She was too thick, in both senses of the word. Too big. Too dim. Too Henrietta.

But there were much worse things to be. She liked her own body, even if the gentlemen of the *ton* did not. It was strong and useful and gave her pleasure. She liked her own mind, even though it was far more interested in people than in books.

Their neighbors, the Ramseys, had also come to town for the Season, and unlike her brother Alexander, Geoffrey did not seem to think he was too young for balls. He politely asked her to dance from time to time, but she could tell it was a duty for him. He danced with plenty of other young ladies—slim, graceful ones—and she had ample opportunity to observe him as he did so. He approached those partners with eagerness and looked at them with what Henrietta guessed was a lustful gleam in his eye, puffing out his chest, getting closer than was proper during a waltz.

When the Season ended, Henrietta had had very few callers, no suitors, and no offers of marriage. And she had only seen Mr. Hartwell once when he had paid a call at the town house during his quarterly trip to the capital. The weather had been dry that day, the curl sadly not in evidence. And, if possible, Mr. Hartwell had looked even thinner than usual. He might waste away without ever once tasting Henrietta's custard.

It was a relief to leave London finally, to pack up and go home. She and her father and her younger brother Gideon were in one carriage and her mother, sisters, and Alexander were in another. And then there were all the carriages for the valets and lady's maids and several wagons for trunks and boxes.

What a lot of fuss and trouble she had made for everyone with no resultant match.

The Stafford carriages were well out of London and Gideon had his nose deep in a book when Henrietta took a deep breath and interrupted her father's amusing story about how the Duke of Thornwick's pantaloons had been soiled by the Duke of Kittredge's dog in the billiards room of their club. While Thornwick was wearing them.

"I'm sorry, Papa."

His bushy orange-brown eyebrows—so like fox tails in miniature, she had always thought—knitted together, furrowing his freckled forehead. "Sorry? For what, Hen?"

"For wasting everyone's time." She tried to laugh. "I don't think I want another Season."

"Nonsense. First, securing your happiness will never be a waste of time for me or your mother. And, of course, you'll have another Season. It's just this particular clutch of young blades are cork-brained. Wait and see. The right man will come along. "

Henrietta gulped. "I hope so."

"And he'll be the luckiest man in England. You're the sweetest of girls with a heart of gold."

"Thank you, Papa."

"And a very fine rider."

Yes, she was. And, at first, being home was wonderful. She rode Zephyr to her heart's content and was happy to be with just her family who liked her very well. Her nineteenth birthday was celebrated at the end of August in the perfect manner with a family dinner and lots of hugs and kisses and her mother recalling fondly how Henrietta had been the easiest and best-tempered baby right from the very beginning, barely crying before settling into her first cuddle with her mama.

However, a shooting party was planned for the end of the

summer. In previous years, Henrietta had enjoyed her parents' house parties and the variety of company they brought, but after her Season, she had had her fill of being on view, of being judged and found wanting.

The Ramseys were to be included in the party, and invitations had been extended to Lord Danforth and his sister Alice, the Duke and Duchess of Abingdon and their three youngest children, and Lord Burchester.

The Earl of Burchester was a merry, talkative, silver-haired man who had danced with Henrietta at a few balls during the Season. She had liked laughing with him. She didn't mind she was taller than he was. Yes, he was old—at least thirty years of age, if not more—but Mr. Hartwell was far older than the earl despite Mr. Hartwell's raven-black hair, and she very much liked Mr. Hartwell, of course.

But before the guests arrived, her mother warned her never to be left alone with Lord Burchester.

"Phineas Edge is not looking for a bride. And I know he's given his word to your father that he would never dally with a maiden, but I've caught him eyeing you a few times."

Well, that was nice. Even if the earl didn't want to get married and she didn't think he'd make a very good husband for her. He was far too silly. Being married to him would be like eating treacle tarts at every meal. Fun at first, but eventually sickening.

The house party proved to be far less unpleasant than she had feared it would be. Despite the many guests, Henrietta had a great deal of liberty to do as she liked.

Lady Phoebe Finch, the Duke of Abingdon's daughter, spent all her time in the library with George Danforth, the pair of them bent over a chessboard as Amelia looked on and issued scathing commentary and Gideon quietly read book after book in the corner. Alice Danforth and Ellen quarreled like a pair of cats and then reconciled and then squabbled again. The Duchess of Abingdon and Lady Ramsey gossiped for hours about the Season and were quite patient when her own mother would try to divert them into a discussion of gnomic verses. Andrew Finch snuck away to the music room, and all the other men went off to hunt every morning.

With everyone else so well-occupied, Henrietta found she could still ride twice a day. As the house party was drawing to a close and she was feeling the flutterings in her stomach she always felt just before a visit from Mr. Hartwell, Henrietta and Geoffrey happened to ride out at the same time one fine September afternoon. She would have rather been alone with Zephyr and her thoughts of Mr. Hartwell, but perhaps Geoffrey had changed his mind about her and now thought she might make a wife. And if she were to marry Geoffrey, she should spend time with him. Shouldn't she?

They rode beside one another, chatting about the weather and the house party. Then, in the midst of boasting to her about the birds he had shot that morning, Geoffrey remarked, "You know, you should be smaller. Your mount could go much faster if you were."

She took his statement as an impersonal observation about riding, so she patted Zephyr's neck and laughed. "Yes, and the same is true for you."

Geoffrey must have abruptly reined in his horse because after a minute or so, she noticed he wasn't next to her any longer. She looked over her shoulder and saw him fuming, far behind her. She turned Zephyr and rode back to him.

"What's wrong?"

He pulled himself up very straight in his saddle. "In case you hadn't noticed, Hen, I am not fat. Not anymore."

He said the word *fat* as if it were a horrible, sinful thing. Like being a traitor or a murderer. And, besides, Geoffrey had never been fat. He'd been a round-cheeked, sturdy boy and now, he was a well-built, muscular man. He didn't have Mr. Hartwell's sharp cheekbones or spare body, but he wasn't fat.

Finally, she realized what his own comment to her had meant. Foolish girl. He was telling her she should be *thinner* when he said *smaller*.

She hung her head, her face hot and pricking with a strange, new shame.

"Forgive me," she mumbled, not knowing what else to say, not knowing if she was apologizing for being too slow to understand him or for being too fat.

Only much later, lying in bed that night, did she think how neither were things that required an apology.

And how her body was none of Geoffrey's business.

But if she married him, it would be.

THREE

Late summer always brought an extra degree of melancholy to Oliver Hartwell. August was the month his second wife had died giving birth to his son, and his first wife had perished on this very day in September, ten years ago.

No wonder he had left Crossthwaite a few days early and pushed on well past nightfall in order to arrive at his friend's house. Tonight was not a night for Oliver Hartwell to be alone.

The duke had warned him by letter that Bexton Manor might still be overrun with shooting party guests, but Oliver hoped this place could still be a haven for him, just as it had been for so many years.

He was comforted as his carriage came down the drive. Despite the late hour, lamplight streamed from at least half a dozen windows, and the house looked as welcoming as ever.

Of course, he would have preferred to have his friend and the Stafford family to himself, to know he might walk with Crispin tomorrow morning, talking over Dalrymple's theory of an undiscovered southern continent. And then an afternoon of whisky in the study and a dinner presided over by the lovely duchess who would discourse on Æthelwad and Ælfthryth and Æthelred while the flock of redheaded children laughed and scrapped good-naturedly.

There was so much life in this house, so different from the quiet shadows of Crossthwaite. No wonder he travelled to London on the flimsiest of pretexts only to have a reason to stop over at Bexton Manor.

Oliver knew most would consider his friendship with Crispin Stafford an unlikely one. They had been at school together but separated by several years. Crispin was a duke, while Oliver could be considered, at best, a somewhat-gentleman farmer with a father whose wealth had come from trade, a mother whose sister had married nobility, a cousin who was a viscount, *et cetera*.

And the characters of the two men were a study in contrasts. Crispin was all ebullient vigor. Oliver was all sedate reserve. Crispin was never alone and always happy. Oliver was always alone and never happy.

Except here.

"Oliver!"

In the front hall of Bexton Manor, Crispin strode forward and shook his hand and then embraced him.

"Welcome, welcome, dear friend. Didn't expect you tonight, but it's no trouble at all, and I am so happy you've arrived. Just let me introduce you to the gentlemen. We're all in here." Crispin guided him towards the billiards room. "Having a tournament. Will you join us? A glass of whisky? Oh, I better keep my voice down. The ladies and children are abed."

Oliver craved distraction, but he didn't think he could tolerate the privileged—dare he say smug?—bonhomie radiating from all the titled gentlemen in the billiards room. Crispin was different, of course, but at the moment Oliver felt far too vulnerable to exchange polite remarks with strangers with whom he could have nothing in common.

After pouring him a glass of whisky and making introductions, Crispin changed his tack. No one ever understood Oliver as well as Crispin did.

"No, after a long journey, I'm sure you want some peace. Shall Catesby show you to your bedchamber? Or will you retire to my study? Stretch out your legs in front of the fire?"

Oliver thanked Crispin for the whisky and said he would make his own way to the study.

"I'll come join you when this lot are done putting balls in pockets," Crispin whispered in his ear as he clapped him on the back.

Those words gave Oliver some succor as he walked to the study, but as soon as he sank down into his accustomed chair, his dark thoughts returned. If he had been in Crispin's company, Oliver might have been able to reason with himself, banish his guilt.

But not when he was alone. Not tonight.

Tonight, he was a wife-killer.

He had married two fragile women—each damaged in different ways—and he was complicit in their deaths.

One wife dead through neglect. He should have known the depths of Violet's unhappiness and found a way to free her instead of burying his head in the sand.

One wife dead from bearing his son. Because he had foisted his desire on Emily. Because he had wanted to bed his wife like a normal husband would. Because he had wanted children and thought he could create something like the chaotic amity of Bexton Manor at Crossthwaite.

He should have known better. Oliver Hartwell was not fit for family, for fathering, for husbanding anything except sheep.

Nathaniel was three years of age now. Sickly like his dead

mother. Silent and withdrawn like his wretch of a father. Fated either for an early death or a lifetime of loneliness.

And Oliver felt powerless to force a change in his son's destiny or his own. He was doomed to stand by and watch as his little boy dwindled and diminished.

He had not cried since his own boyhood, but in this familiar chair, alone in the one place where he had found friendship and affection, Oliver abandoned himself to self-pity and despair.

He drained his whisky and wept.

Henrietta threw the counterpane to the side. She couldn't find sleep and the longer she lay in her bed, the farther away it seemed. She kept thinking of what Geoffrey had said this afternoon.

She was dwelling on it, and Henrietta was not a dweller.

She sat up. She needed company. Ellen and Amelia and her mother had surely fallen asleep long ago. There was nothing for it except a visit to Zephyr.

She lit a lamp. Should she dress? No. Just a dressing gown over her nightdress and she would lace up her boots. None of the guests would be about this late at night. She'd nip out to the stables, quicker than lightning.

She crept from her room and descended the stairs. On the next floor down, she saw light coming from under the door of her father's study. Papa was up. They could play draughts. That would be even more comforting than a visit to Zephyr. She might mention what Geoffrey had said, and her father would tell her what to make of it.

She opened the study door and saw a figure in a chair, dark head bent, narrow shoulders shaking, and immediately knew to whom the head and shoulders belonged.

Mr. Hartwell. He had arrived!

Her niggling little hurt was instantly blotted out by the excitement she always felt in his presence. True, she had been holding back her most fetching dinner dress for his first night at Bexton Manor and now he was going to see her wearing her oldest dressing gown and boots, her hair in a messy plait. Of course, it wouldn't make any difference to him how she looked, but her own vanity suffered a small sting. Only a small one, though, because it was just so wonderful Mr. Hartwell was here.

He raised his head, and the light from the fire revealed the tears streaming down his cheeks.

It was as she had always suspected. Mr. Hartwell felt very deeply. His manner might be restrained, but that was because he felt so much and so strongly, he had no choice but to tamp down all his emotions lest he be swept away by them.

She put her lamp down and rushed to him and even though he was already rising to his feet, she seized both his hands and dragged him back down into the chair and went to her knees on the carpet in front of him.

"I'm sorry you're so sad, Mr. Hartwell. I wish you wouldn't be."

"I—" He tried to remove his hands from hers, but she held him fast.

"You must miss Mrs. Hartwell terribly."

His face was shadowed. "I—please—"

"I can't allow you to cry alone. I'm sure your grief is too much to bear."

"This isn't…you must go, Lady—" He mumbled something. "Or I must go. Please let me stand."

She looked down to where she had clasped his hands, holding them so tightly his fingers were white.

"Oh. Oh, yes."

She let go of him and got to her feet with difficulty, her boots tangling in her nightdress. He unfolded his long, thin body from the chair and rose with far more dignity than she had.

He kept his head down. "Please forgive me. A momentary weakness."

He walked away from the fire, giving her his back. From the movements of his arms, she guessed he was taking out a handkerchief and wiping away his tears.

He turned, and although his face was now dry, his wet lashes clung to each other, ebony spikes rimming his reddened eyes. She'd known him her whole life, and she'd never noticed his long, sooty eyelashes. Such a softness in the middle of that austere face, those chiseled cheekbones, that angled jaw and pointed chin. How could she have missed his eyelashes before?

"I hope you can forget this unfortunate circumstance. I will retire now, so you can have the use of the study."

"The use of…? Oh, no, I only came in here because I saw the light. I was on my way to the stables." She lifted her dressing gown and nightdress to show him her boots.

"Ah," he said and raised his dark eyebrows.

It was the first time Mr. Hartwell had ever raised his eyebrows at her. She couldn't think. Her breath got short. She waited for him to say something more, not wanting to leave yet, needing to make sure he was truly all right.

The air in the room felt very hot and close.

Finally, he bowed again and said, "Well, still, you must excuse me." He moved towards the door.

She couldn't let their encounter end this way. Here, at last, was her chance to help him. But her words had vanished and there was no custard to hand.

She darted forward and hugged him.

He shuddered but did not resist. He let her embrace his lean body and pin his long arms to his sides.

She looked up at him and said the only thing she could think of—the truth.

"I want you to be happy."

Her beautiful, young, strong, healthy, decidedly female body against Oliver's. Her breasts, her belly, her thighs.

She was one of the Stafford daughters. The oldest one. The tallest one. The gorgeous one. The one he had suddenly noticed for the first time in London a few months ago. *Noticed*, as a man notices a woman. Her flawless figure, her winsome face, her bright smile. But he had told himself to avert his eyes, that part of his life was over, he was a lecher, she was a child, she was his friend's daughter, for God's sake.

In fact, he had done such a good job of pushing her out of his mind that suddenly he couldn't remember her name. It had slipped away. What did everyone call her? Duck? Goose? *Hen*.

She looked up at him, her eyes shining in sympathy, and told him she wanted him to be happy.

He was doing his best to rebuild his stoic façade, but her words made him want to sob again. What generous hearts these Staffords had! And, in contrast, what a pitiful, mean creature he was, crying for himself.

She tried to get closer to him and stepped on his shoes. This made her stumble and he had to catch her to keep her from falling, and she burst into laughter. She was so pretty, so rosy and sweet as she laughed in his arms that he quite lost his head.

Those pink lips. That warm breath with the scent of sugared violets. He wanted those lips, that breath. That delight, that promise. That hope. That kindness.

This soft, abundant, feminine flesh and these shimmering locks of fire.

He pulled her closer, bent his head, and kissed her laughing mouth.

She stopped laughing. She stopped doing anything at all. She was immobile. A heated, statuesque goddess against him. Her lips tender and pliant and seemingly made for his.

A hunger he had long thought dead rose up in him. He wanted her naked, underneath him, begging him to take her. He wanted his face buried in her voluptuous breasts, his hands on her lush bottom, his cock in her cunt. He wanted her with a ruthless savagery that knew no reason.

His depraved thoughts surging, his mouth still joined to hers and his arms still locked around her, he heard the library door open and his friend's shocked gasp.

"Oliver. Henrietta."

Henrietta. The girl in his arms was Henrietta.

But even as her name branded itself on his heart and his cock, the animal part of his brain would not allow him to release her.

Mine.

She was the one who pushed him away and put a distance between them.

"Papa, I fell and Mr. Hartwell saved me."

A slow dawning.

Something deplorable had just occurred and he was the agent of it. Oliver took two halting steps away from Henrietta and turned and bowed to Crispin.

"Your Grace."

When he straightened from the bow, he saw Danforth, Burchester, Ramsey, and Ramsey's son standing behind his friend.

His muzzy head whirred and clicked like his old viameter as he grappled with the immense ramifications of the kiss he had just stolen.

Damn, damn, damn, damn. Damn you to hell, Oliver Hartwell.

If it had been only Crispin who had found them thus, the

situation might be salvaged for the girl. Oliver would have lost the duke's trust—and almost certainly, his friendship—and that would be a lethal blow. The worst thing he could imagine. The end of everything good in his life. But only for him. No harm would come to Lady Henrietta.

But for her to be discovered in the arms of a man in the middle of the night in front of witnesses outside the family? A scandal of the worst kind.

Poor girl. He had ruined her as he had ruined everything and everyone else in his life.

Oliver glanced quickly at Henrietta. Her whole face was red, making the freckles that dotted her snub nose disappear.

"Papa, you aren't angry, are you? I was on my way to the stables."

The duke turned to the other men. "If you'll excuse us."

"Certainly," Lord Ramsey huffed, and the four men disappeared.

"Henrietta, go to your bedchamber. Now. Mr. Hartwell and I must talk."

"No, no— What are you going to talk about? You mustn't think, I just wanted to, I mean, I saw the light in the study." Henrietta poked a foot out from under her nightdress. "See? I have boots on. I'm going out to the stables."

"Hen. Your bedchamber. Now."

The girl chewed her lip and scurried from the room.

The duke closed the door but did not turn around. Instead, he put his forehead and both hands on the wide oak slab as if the ancient wood could lend him strength.

Oliver took a deep breath. "Lady Henrietta is innocent in this matter." His voice cracked. "She happened upon me, and she did fall, and I did catch her, and I was the one who took advantage."

Crispin finally pushed away from the door and began pacing, running both hands through his red hair.

"Shit, shit, shit. Of all men, I would have never thought you— How could you, Oliver?"

He didn't know. Even now, it was inconceivable to him that he had kissed his friend's daughter.

"I— I have no excuse. I am unworthy, but I will, of course, offer for your daughter's hand."

"This is a hell of a thing. The gossip will be sickening."

"I hope you believe Lady Henrietta was not at fault here. I am entirely to blame."

Crispin finally faced Oliver. The duke radiated fury, his fists clenched tightly at his sides, his brow thunderous, his eyes flashing with a murderous, green fire.

"Of course, she's not at fault. She doesn't have a devious bone in her body. Couldn't lay a plan to trap a man if her life depended on it."

Oliver steeled himself for a blow, but suddenly the duke's rage drained away and his broad shoulders slumped. It was a monstrous thing to see Crispin reduced and defeated this way.

And Oliver had been the cause.

When Crispin spoke again, it was an anguished mutter. "I will go wake my wife. Maybe she'll have some idea of what to do. Because, at this moment, I can think of no solution except—"

Crispin cut himself short as he flung the door open and strode from the room, cursing.

Except, Oliver was sure he had been about to say, *giving my precious daughter away to a man who wouldn't know the first thing about treating a wife well.*

Henrietta fretted. There was no question of sleep. Something terrible was going to happen.

Perhaps it could all be hushed up? She had heard whispers about other young ladies being compromised and ruined. But that hadn't been what had been going on. Not at all.

Poor Mr. Hartwell, having to face her father's anger. When it was her fault.

But she never could have let him cry alone. She never could have let him leave the room without trying to make him feel better.

And she couldn't regret she had had her first kiss. And for that first kiss to have come from Mr. Hartwell? For her to have wished for him to be happy and he had decided what would make him happy was kissing her? Such things didn't happen to Henrietta. It was a kiss out of someone else's life.

She put her fingers to her mouth. How idiotic she had been. Turning to stone like that, not knowing what to do. Not taking advantage of those brief seconds of closeness. Not kissing him back. If only she had been paying better attention while it was happening. The memory of the sensation was already fading, and she wanted to grab it and hold it tightly so she could remember the kiss forever.

After what seemed hours and just when she was on the verge of falling sleep while sitting up on the edge of her bed, her mother swept in without knocking, wringing her hands, her usual dreamy vagueness nowhere to be seen.

"Are you all right, my darling girl?"

"Yes."

"Oh, Hen, I'm so sorry. I've failed you."

"No, Mama. What do you mean?"

Her mother tilted Henrietta's chin up and examined her. "Dear heart, you are so much like your father, all impulsive passion and tenderness. And I love that about both of you, so I never taught you to guard against it."

"But I didn't do anything wrong, I promise. And neither did Mr. Hartwell. Not really, I don't think. It was just a kiss."

Her mother sighed and sat down on the edge of the bed

beside her. "In this stupid, modern age and in the idiotically narrow-minded circles we move in, there's no such thing as *just a kiss*. There should be, but there isn't. And it's all made worse because the kiss was in front of the Ramseys and the other gentlemen. With you in your nightdress. Mr. Hartwell understands how it must appear. He immediately offered for your hand to spare you scandal."

"But he's still mourning his wife, Mama. He doesn't want to marry me!"

"He has taken responsibility and is quite ashamed he might have caused you harm—"

"He didn't harm me!"

"Your reputation, Hen."

"I don't care about my reputation. I just don't want Papa to be angry with Mr. Hartwell. Will they still be friends? Does Papa know Mr. Hartwell didn't do anything wrong and this is all my fault?"

Her mother smiled sadly and stroked Henrietta's hair. "Your father understands men because he is one."

"Mama—"

"But your father has also lived nineteen years with you. He knows how you're apt to do things out of the goodness of your heart without a thought for the consequences."

Henrietta had *had* a thought. Her thought had been that Mr. Hartwell was crying and she might comfort him. True, she hadn't thought much beyond that. She certainly hadn't thought of a kiss. A kiss from Mr. Hartwell was the stuff of secret, impossible dreams.

Let alone an offer of marriage.

Henrietta bent her neck to lean her head on her much shorter mother's shoulder. "What's going to happen now?"

"I want you to sleep for a bit, if you can. All right? Then, when you wake up, you can hear what Mr. Hartwell has to say, and you and I and your father will have a confab. Don't worry, dearest. We love you, and we would never force you to do anything you didn't want to do."

But what did Henrietta want to do? What did she want, besides everyone to be happy?

Everyone.

But especially Mr. Hartwell.

FOUR

Even though only a few hours remained until dawn, Crispin went to his wife's bedchamber and stripped off his clothes and crawled into the bed beside Georgiana. He needed to be with her. He needed the comfort of her body, the wisdom of her words.

She put her book aside and turned into his embrace, and he rested his chin on top of her head.

"Oliver is a very lucky man," his wife said, her cheek against the ginger pelt on his chest.

Crispin snorted. "Lucky I didn't throttle him."

Georgiana pulled away from him, something she almost never did. She stared up at him with the big, blue eyes that always undid him.

"Don't say that. He's your friend. And a threat like that is beneath you, Bey."

Yes, his wife liked when he became her savage Beowulf during their love-making, but she had high expectations for how he conducted himself as a civilized father and a duke.

He tugged her back into his arms. "Yes, of course, I

wouldn't have killed him, sweetling." He paused. "But it's a good thing Alexander wasn't there. I'll have to get to the boy first thing and calm him down, tell him Oliver has offered for Hen's hand."

Georgiana sighed. The heir's hot temper was a frequent source of worry for both of them, and they often discussed their hope that Alexander would mellow with age. But, so far, no luck. The young man was still a veritable petard, ready to go off with very little provocation.

"Yes, please. No duels. Oliver will let Alexander kill him and that would break his sister's heart."

Oliver didn't have a sister. Crispin frowned. "Whose heart?"

Georgiana rolled onto her back and stared up at the canopy. "Hen's."

Crispin should be well-used to feeling he was three steps behind his wife's nimble brain, but her quick leaps still surprised him.

"Why would Hen's heart be broken?"

Georgiana reached out and brought his hand to her mouth and kissed the knuckle that had a scar on it from when he had knocked out the tooth of his archenemy.

"We'll try to get as much sleep as we can this morning, and the four of us will go to the bishop tomorrow morning. An ordinary license. Then they can be married in a sennight."

Georgiana must have already decided the issue was settled and Henrietta should accept Oliver. Crispin hoped he could come around to his wife's way of thinking, but a marriage between his friend and his daughter still seemed unnatural to him. Perverse. A mismatch of the most grievous kind. And not just because of the difference in their ages, but because of Oliver's dark past. And because his sunshine daughter was all un-blighted innocence. Until tonight.

Shit.

He needed to get to the bottom of why his wife was so calmly accepting of this marriage while he was still tormented.

"Why did you say Oliver was lucky?"

She closed her eyes. "If you could pick a wife for your friend, what would she be like?"

Crispin thought of Oliver's first wife and shuddered. His greatest regret might be introducing his friend to Miss Violet Winter. Then he thought over what little he knew of Oliver's second wife, the former Miss Emily Wilkes.

Neither of those women had ever given Oliver anything close to what Crispin had with Georgiana. The largest stroke of good fortune in Crispin's very lucky life had come over two decades ago when the most desirable woman he had ever seen also turned out to be the love of his life.

"Bey?"

He squeezed her hand. "I'd pick someone like you. Beautiful, loving, caring, capable, thoughtful, honest."

She rolled towards him, keeping ahold of his hand, clasping it to her bosom. "And I'd pick someone like you. Someone who likes him. Someone who is full of fun and vim. Someone who is all heart and fair play. You are his friend, after all, and that's what a wife should be, first and foremost."

Crispin might not share his wife's genius, but he wasn't stupid. Georgiana was saying Henrietta was a combination of the two of them and would make a good wife for Oliver.

He pushed a stray blonde curl behind his brilliant wife's ear. "But the more important question is whether Oliver will be a good husband for our Hen."

Georgiana gave him a soulful look, the kind she couldn't help but give when she pitied Crispin's lack of understanding.

"She answered that question for herself a long time ago, Bey. She wants him. Haven't you seen the way she looks at him?"

Crispin was astounded. "What?"

"She has only ever had eyes for him."

"A long time?"

"Five years or so."

Crispin had no idea girls could be interested in men while they were still so young.

Georgiana smiled wistfully. "During her Season, I worried she would never be happy with another. No one seemed to please her. So, at least, this puts one of my fears to rest."

Crispin was still struggling with the idea that his little girl might *want* a man. An adult man. A man his age. His friend.

"You have to tell me if Ellen and Amelia have set their caps for anyone. Lord Marsburn, maybe?" Lord Marsburn was in his ninth decade.

Georgiana giggled. "Amelia, I think, will be a late bloomer like her mother. Remember I thought I should have been a nun in the Middle Ages until I met you?"

"And Ellen?"

Another deep sigh. "I love Ellen, of course, but she's pure trouble with a capitalized, illuminated *T*. I can't start worrying about Ellen right now, Bey, or I'll never get to sleep."

"Yes, no need. There'll be plenty of time for that in the years to come. And as always, we'll muddle through it together. Go to sleep, wife."

He turned down the wick on the lamp and punched his pillow a few times as Georgiana rolled away from him. But it was only to pull off her nightdress and settle into her favorite position for sleeping. On her side, scooted back against him, her naked, plump bottom resting on his groin, her back against his chest, drawing his arm around her soft waist so they were coiled together as tightly as two people could be.

Thank God he had his duchess to explain things to him. Maybe this marriage between his friend and his daughter would not turn out to be the ill-fated, deviant thing he had thought it would be.

And perhaps Henrietta would somehow put right the wrong done to Oliver by her parents, long ago.

Five

At noon, Henrietta went out to the grounds with her mother. Mr. Hartwell was waiting for them in the rose garden, which looked rather sad since all the blooms were fading and there would be no more new ones this year.

Mr. Hartwell removed his hat and bowed. "Your Grace. Lady Henrietta."

Henrietta couldn't look at him. She couldn't. She was the one who had put him in this awful position.

"If you please, I would like to speak to Lady Henrietta alone."

Her usually indulgent, kind mother used her sternest voice. "There's been quite enough being alone already, don't you think?"

"I would wish for you to see us at all times, Your Grace, just not to hear us. It's important Lady Henrietta speak freely."

"My daughter knows she can speak freely in front of me."

"Then I would like to speak freely. Please, Georgiana."

Her mother finally seemed to remember Mr. Hartwell was

a friend and gave a reluctant nod and plopped herself down on a bench and opened her parasol. Mr. Hartwell offered Henrietta his arm. She took it, but she still couldn't look at him.

After they had strolled down the gravel path a good ways away from her mother, he said, "This is unfortunate."

Henrietta continued to stare straight ahead. "I'm so sorry, Mr. Hartwell. I hope my father was not angry with you. It was all my doing, and I was trying to tell him that. It's not fair, at all."

"It is an injustice that a young woman might be forced to marry to save her reputation. Especially when she is blameless."

"Oh, but I am to blame! I am always doing hopelessly stupid things."

He said stiffly, "You were trying to be kind to your father's friend. That is all. I was the one who committed an unforgivable obscenity upon you. Without your permission."

His kiss was *not* an obscenity. And, of course, she would have said yes if he had asked to kiss her. She looked at his face finally—the dark circles under his eyes, the deeply etched grooves by his mouth—and tried to think of a way to correct him without being impolite, but he was already speaking again.

"In reparation, I pledge to protect you in any way I can, including offering for your hand. But the decision is yours, Lady Henrietta. You need not marry me. The scandal might fade in time, and you might make a match with someone more suitable."

Was this a proposal? Henrietta swallowed. "I have had a Season already, you know."

"You have?" He darted a look at her. "You're a girl."

How could he say that when there was nothing girlish about her? Tall, full-figured, and, in passing, often thought to be years older than she really was. She tossed her head, willing him to see her hair was up, not down.

"I have just become nineteen years of age. I share a birthday with your son."

His dark eyebrows went up. "I see."

"I was not popular during my Season. I am…I am too big. The fashion is for small, slender ladies."

The eyebrows climbed even higher. "Is it?"

"And I'm not clever or funny."

He did not contradict her. She felt more of a great lump than ever, but she wanted him to know he had not ruined her chances. They were already ruined. Nil, in fact.

"So, no matter what, I don't think it likely I'll find a husband." Then a thought occurred to her. "Except a fortune-hunter who might want my dowry."

His posture became even more rigid. "If you do me the honor of becoming my wife, I will arrange for a generous jointure from my own assets. Your dowry and the accumulated income will be held in trust separately and will also go to you in its entirety upon my death."

"Your death?" She clutched at his arm. "Are you ill?"

"No. But I am twenty-two years older than you. God willing, I'll die before you."

She whispered, "Your other wives died before you."

He turned away.

"I'm sorry, I'm sorry," she cried out, despairing over her own thoughtlessness. "I shouldn't have mentioned that. Of course, you'll die before me."

But what a terrible thing. Mr. Hartwell, dead. She couldn't bear to think of it.

His voice was without emotion. "If you accept me, you will want for nothing. I will provide everything for you, including ample pin money. As I said, your dowry would remain untouched."

So, this *was* her proposal. All talk of money and death. Not at all how she had imagined it. But she'd never dared imagine it would be Mr. Hartwell asking for her hand.

Everything was so higgledy-piggledy in her mind right now. She must get some orderly picture of what her life would be like. *As his wife.* Even thinking the words made her heart thump wildly.

"Would I live with you?"

"As you wish. It might be best if you did, at first, in order to quell gossip. But after a time, you might want to live elsewhere. My home is in a quiet place, and you might find the countryside not to your liking. I could buy a house in town for your use."

She shook her head. "Oh, no. No. I have no fondness for London."

"Ho, there!"

The shout came from across the rose garden. It was Geoffrey, half-walking, half-running, his boots crunching loudly on the gravel. He arrived out of breath and bowed to Henrietta, pointedly ignoring Mr. Hartwell.

"I must speak to you, Hen. Immediately."

She looked at Mr. Hartwell nervously before answering Geoffrey. "We are in the middle of an important conversation."

"What I need to say to you is far more important than anything this—" Geoffrey's lip curled in a sneer, "*gentleman* could have to say to you."

He seized her wrist roughly and pulled her away from Mr. Hartwell.

"Come along, Hen."

As she trotted in Geoffrey's wake, she gazed back over her shoulder. Mr. Hartwell stood, head bowed, a lonely, tall figure. As always, she felt an inexplicable tug in her belly towards him, a yearning to be close to him.

"Keep up."

A wrench on her arm and now she was quite put out with Geoffrey and his rudeness.

"What is it?" she demanded.

"I am willing to marry you," Geoffrey said angrily, still striding forward, his face red. "On the condition you give me your word you will behave with the utmost propriety going forward. Or there will be consequences."

Henrietta bridled. She wasn't a child to be threatened. Or punished. This was not how her father treated her mother, not how a husband treated a wife.

"And my father says if your father increases your dowry and includes the unentailed land next to the Ramsey barony, we can be wed quickly."

She wouldn't be Geoffrey's honored bride, but a bargaining chip for money and land. She felt so dirty, just like the earth she was being traded for.

"And you must promise me you will make an effort with your appearance."

She *always* made an effort with her appearance. Even with all this tumult, she had bathed and chosen a pretty gown this morning, had sat quietly for Lucy to arrange her hair. But recalling yesterday afternoon, she knew Geoffrey meant something else.

"I should try to become *smaller*?" She used his own word deliberately. "I should try to look more like my sister?"

Geoffrey snorted. "I suppose Amelia is an acceptable size, and Ellen is all right from the waist up, but she's far too big—" He gestured at Henrietta's lower half.

Amelia was small and lithe, but she was barely thirteen! And Ellen was a beauty, already greatly admired even though she wasn't out yet, sure to have many offers of marriage when the time came for her first Season.

Ellen was perfect. *Perfect.*

A rage started to simmer inside Henrietta. How dare Geoffrey talk about her sisters that way, as if they were made up of parts that either pleased or displeased him? As if that were the purpose of their bodies?

Geoffrey's next words had a bite of menace to them. "But if you don't marry right away, neither of them will ever nab a husband."

She halted and pulled her arm out of Geoffrey's grasp. "What do you mean?"

He stopped walking, too, and faced her with a shrug. "Oh, you know."

"No, I don't. What do you mean?"

"Don't be a dunce, Hen. Scandal with one daughter spreads to the others. You must know everyone in the *ton* will think Ellen and Amelia are trollops."

Like you were the words he left unsaid.

But her mother had told her she didn't have to…oh, no. Never mind about herself. That wondrous kiss from Mr. Hartwell had ruined Ellen's and Amelia's matrimonial chances, too.

She looked at Geoffrey, the only man she had ever thought she might have a possibility of marrying. But he didn't love her. He didn't even like her. She would disappoint him. Already, she resented he didn't want her as she was.

And Geoffrey was…Geoffrey was…

Her anger boiled over and all the bad words she knew spewed into her brain.

Geoffrey was a beastly, boorish, bloody bully of an arse.

She looked back at Mr. Hartwell, still standing at the far end of the rose garden, hat in hand, waiting. He was, and had always been, a fixed ideal in her mind. It must mean something that she had always been drawn to him. That she had always desired his happiness.

Could she make Mr. Hartwell happy?

She didn't know. But she could try. And this might be her only chance to snatch some future happiness for herself.

She remembered her manners.

"No, thank you," she blurted to Geoffrey. She picked up her skirts and ran all the way back to Mr. Hartwell. She gasped for air and her chest heaved as she stood in front of him in the sunshine.

"Yes. Yes, I'll marry you."

His grave face did not change. "Very well." He bowed and replaced his hat and offered her his arm. "Shall we go tell your parents?"

Six

The guests had all departed a week ago in a welter of whispers about her and Mr. Hartwell's indiscretion and subsequent betrothal. Had it been Geoffrey or his father or one of the other men who had tittle-tattled? She would never know, and it didn't matter.

Henrietta would wed Mr. Hartwell tomorrow.

In the unusually warm September dusk, they strolled the lower lawn, just the two of them. Henrietta's parents had not insisted on a chaperone this evening. They must think the horse was already well out of the stable.

A horse in a stable. How would Zephyr like the Lake District? Because, of course, she would bring her friend with her. She must ask Mr. Hartwell about accommodations for her big horse at Crossthwaite.

But Mr. Hartwell interrupted the silence between them before she could voice her question.

"I will not impose on you."

She had no idea what he meant, so she played with her fan and waited for him to explain himself.

After a bit of time, he said, "I don't know how much your

mother has told you about what passes between a husband and wife."

Henrietta now held her fan up in front of her face to hide her blush and her smile. Her mother was a scholar of the Middle Ages and back in those olden days, people had been quite frank about things that most ladies today would consider unmentionable. The unconventional duchess had adopted that same frankness. Henrietta had been well-prepared for the changes in her body, the beginning of her courses, the blossoming of her own desire.

Of course, Henrietta had never wanted to listen to most of what her mother had to say on the subject of *what passes between a husband and a wife* because it often involved Mama rhapsodizing about Papa and…ew.

But Henrietta knew plenty, and she had learned some on her own. She was a horse girl. She knew about mating. Breeding. And she knew she wanted something more than her own touch.

"I am familiar with my marital duty." That had been the phrase she had heard bandied about in hushed tones by other young ladies during her come-out in London.

They had reached the ha-ha, and Mr. Hartwell looked down into it as if examining the stones for cracks.

"We will be married because of my folly. As your husband, I will do all I can to make amends to you. But you owe me nothing. There is no need for us to engage in…I will not visit your bedchamber, so there is no need for you to feel any anxiety on that front."

Oh.

Despite his kiss, he didn't want her.

But couldn't he make do with her? She had all the necessary parts. In the dark, under bedclothes, he might be able to ignore what he saw as her failings since she would be his wife, ready to hand.

But he was not even going to try. Would he take a mistress?

"You don't have needs?" Her mother had spoken of masculine needs. And feminine needs, too, but Henrietta knew all about those already.

"No."

But he had a son. So he had performed his own marital duty with at least one of his wives. Henrietta must be hideous in his eyes. Unwomanly. Grotesque.

He finally met her eyes. "I did not mean to embarrass you with my clumsiness on the subject. I just did not want you to be fearful. So, I thought it would be best if I were forthright."

She hadn't been fearful. She had been excited. How many young women found themselves engaged to marry the man who had been the object of all of their girlhood fantasies?

But it was good he had been forthright. So she would not wait in her bed tomorrow night for him to come to her. To touch her and maybe kiss her again. To induct her into the mysteries of human copulation.

To share that great intimacy with her.

For the first time in a long time, her eyes smarted on her own behalf rather than someone else's. She had been cheated out of affection and admiration. Of being someone's choice. And now to discover she would also be cheated out of giving and receiving pleasure?

But she mustn't cry like a silly girl in front of him. She was going to be a wife. *His* wife. And it was good he had been forthright and abolished misunderstanding between them. There should be no misunderstandings between husbands and wives.

"Yes. Thank you, Mr. Har— May I call you Oliver?"

That would be something. To use his name. *Oliver.* Despite the heat, she shivered as a thrill ran through her body.

"As you wish." He bowed his head. "My lady."

Oh. No.

"I don't want to be a lady. Couldn't I be Henrietta to you and Mrs. Hartwell to everyone else?"

He raised his eyebrows. "You are a duke's daughter. Of course, you should keep your title."

"Why? Do you not want…I mean, if I were to be Mrs. Hartwell, the same name as your other wives, would that upset you?"

"Your parents would be disappointed if you gave up your title."

"But you…" She faltered. "How would *you* feel? Do you want a wife who is a lady? Is that important to you? I want to be of use to you and if my title is of use, I'll be Lady Henrietta."

The eyebrows lowered. "You needn't worry about being of use to me."

More disappointment. Was she going to be allowed to do anything for him? With him? Maybe she should have accepted Geoffrey's offer. At least, she would have known she had some value, then.

No, your dowry and Bexton land would have been of value to Geoffrey. You would have been…what was the opposite of value? A burden. An overly-large burden.

Her future husband broke into her thoughts. "You should be addressed how you wish to be addressed."

"If it doesn't bother you, I wish to be Mrs. Hartwell, Oliver," she said slowly, savoring his name, loving how the *v* made her upper teeth touch her lower lip for just a moment. "And you must call me by my given name."

"Henrietta."

"Yes." She smiled, feeling a bit better. "Yes, I like that very much. What do you want your son to call me?"

"Nathaniel is three years of age."

She laughed. "He must call me something."

"Whatever you prefer."

"Perhaps Nathaniel might come to call me Mama?"

His face became granite, his voice harsh. "No. Not that. You are not his mother."

Oafish, blundering Henrietta. She had overstepped. "Of course. Yes."

"I do not expect you to mother Nathaniel. You have no obligation towards him. You are only sixteen years older than he is. You could be…"

Had he been about to say *sister and brother*? And he could be her father? Henrietta already had a father; she didn't want another one.

She took a deep breath. This was of the utmost importance, and she must say it now.

"I will be married to Nathaniel's father. Of course, I have an obligation to your child."

And to be a stepmother would be *something*.

He nodded once—a reluctant concession, she thought— but said nothing. Even after all these years, his face was still unreadable to her. What was he thinking?

If only she could come to know his thoughts, then she might learn what made him happy. And then she could do or arrange or be whatever that was. She could become of value to him that way.

That was it. She must solve the mystery that was Mr. Oliver Hartwell. After all, she would have endless opportunities now. No more waiting outside her father's study, sneaking glances at a dark curl. She would have so much time to discover…him.

Like her mother, she would make a thorough study of the subject and unravel it, bit by bit, until it became clear. But, unlike her mother, Henrietta's subject would not be Bede or *Beowulf* or Brunanburh. It would be her husband.

Part Two
A Study in Oliver

Seven

The Lake District.

Henrietta had not been able to stop herself from gasping and cooing and exclaiming in admiration at the passing scenery as they came closer and closer to their destination.

What a beautiful place. All lakes and green fields and hills and mountains. No, hills and mountains weren't right. They were fells, Oliver had said. And the lakes were meres.

From time to time, she looked over at him to see if she was bothering him with her outbursts. She was studying him, as she had promised herself she would.

But Oliver did not appear irritated. True, she had not even known he *could* be irritated until yesterday when she had seen a bit of temper—a raised voice, the twitch of a muscle in his jaw, his eyebrows in a dark *V*—when he thought one of the ostlers at an inn was not gentle enough in his handling of Zephyr.

It had delighted her.

But there was no evidence of disapproval at the moment. True, it was too much to hope for him to smile back at her, but his gray eyes were calm and peaceful.

"This place is lovely," she ventured.

"Yes," he said, his gaze drifting to the window of the carriage. "I think so, too."

Nestled into a little valley, Crossthwaite was also beautiful. A sprawling house, added on to over the years so now it was quite large. And only Oliver and his young son lived here?

"It's originally Tudor," he told her as he helped her down from the carriage. "But there have been improvements made, both before and after I purchased it, and I hope you'll find it adequate."

He was very patient, making sure the grooms knew she wanted to lead Zephyr into the stables herself. After letting her fuss over settling her horse, Oliver took her into the house and made introductions to the rest of the staff. He must have sent word of his marriage because no one seemed surprised to have a new mistress. He then took her on a tour of the rooms on the ground floor before suggesting she must want to rest before dinner.

Not fatigued in the slightest but eager to please, she climbed the stairs. On the landing, she stopped in front of a portrait of a woman with pale skin, fine bones, and enormous, dark eyes. Dark hair like Oliver. And beautiful, like him.

"Is this your sister?"

"I have no sister. This was my second wife. Nathaniel's mother."

Oh. The woman in the painting was ethereal. Exquisitely delicate. So very much Henrietta's opposite in every way. She heard Oliver step onto the landing behind her, come closer to her.

She couldn't think. She blurted, "I'm sorry."

I'm sorry you had to marry me because I wouldn't leave you alone. I'm sorry, I'm sorry, I'm sorry.

"I'm sorry…your wife died. She was beautiful. You must miss her a great deal."

He said nothing.

"And Nathaniel must miss her?"

"He never knew her. She died giving birth."

Henrietta knew that. She meant the child must miss a mother? A motherly influence? She turned her head to look at Oliver, but he was staring at the painting.

"Emily was frail," he said.

"I'm not frail." Another blurt.

His head moved, and he took her in as if seeing her for the first time. "No, you're not."

"Is there a portrait of your first wife, too?"

His face closed, his eyes shuttered. "No."

"I see."

The air was a bit damp, so the curl was dangling. Shiny and soft. Tempting. She could reach out and touch it. But she mustn't. She should not impose herself, either.

"Where's the nursery? I'd so very much like to meet Nathaniel."

Oliver looked up the stairs. "He might be resting."

"Oh, please may I have a peek at him? I can creep away quietly if he's asleep."

After a pause, her husband nodded and took her up another flight of stairs and down a hallway. He stood in an open doorway for a moment and then gestured for her to approach.

Inside what must be the nursery, a dark-haired, dark-eyed little boy sat in a chair that was much too big for him, at a table that was much too high for him. He listlessly pushed blocks around on the table top, every once in a while looking up at his nurse who was in the chair next to him, darning a small stocking.

"Hello." Henrietta used her softest voice which still sounded too loud in this quiet room in this quiet house.

The little boy's head turned and his eyes immediately fixed on his father. The nurse hastily got to her feet and bobbed.

"Sir. Madam."

"Nurse Witherspoon, this is Mrs. Hartwell. Your new mistress."

The nurse bobbed again as Henrietta stepped into the room and curtsied. "I am very pleased to meet you, Nurse Witherspoon."

"And this is Nathaniel," said Oliver.

Henrietta came closer to the table and sank down onto her knees, making her face level with the boy's.

"Hello, Nathaniel. My name is Henrietta, but my brothers and sisters call me Hen. You can call me Hen, too, if you like, because Henrietta is a very long name. Almost as long as Nathaniel." Oh, goodness, she was talking too much.

The boy's eyes were still on his father. She looked over her shoulder at Oliver and smiled. "Nathaniel looks just like his mother."

"Yes," he said briefly.

Henrietta turned back to Nathaniel. "Do you want me to help you get down so you can go hug your father?"

The little boy shifted his gaze to her for the first time but did not answer. Perhaps she should ask a different question. A simpler one.

"Are you playing with blocks?"

The boy did not move or nod or speak or smile or do anything she would have expected a three-year-old child to do. She quite clearly remembered her own brother Gideon when he had been three. How much he had talked and wiggled!

"May I play with you?"

The boy looked at his father once more.

Henrietta tried again. "May I play with your blocks?"

The boy looked back at her. The trace of a nod. Henrietta

took that as a *yes* and moved a bit closer to the table and put one block on top of another.

"I'm building a castle for a king. What are you building?"

The boy reached out and touched one of his blocks. Henrietta selected a block far away from the one he had chosen and put it on her pile.

"I want to build a tall castle. Do you think you could help me?"

The boy's hand tightened on his block, and he brought it towards him. A little shake of his head.

"It's very hard to build a castle." Henrietta put a fourth block on her pile, deliberately placing it off-center, making the pile precarious. "But if I make a mistake, I'll just start again." She put a fifth block on the pile. The top three blocks fell off the pile and hit the table with a clatter.

Nathaniel shrank back.

Had she frightened him? She must show him there was no reason for alarm. She laughed and put her hand to her mouth. "Oops. But no matter. You could teach me. Show me how you build a tall tower with your blocks."

Just like his father, the little boy raised his dark eyebrows at her.

She put a block on top of the two blocks that were still stacked. "Oh, now I think that will stay. What do you think?"

Henrietta turned around to see if Oliver would agree with her, if he would come forward and encourage his son to play with her, but the doorway was empty. He had gone.

Eight

He could not bear to watch the beautiful child he had just married play with his own child.

She was so lovely that it hurt.

Henrietta's ease and frolicsome nature contrasted so sharply with Nathaniel's reticence and solemnity. And his own. Yes, these qualities—along with her sprightly curiosity— could just be part and parcel of her youth, but he didn't think so. All the Staffords possessed these traits in varying degrees.

And observing her physical perfection was akin to torture. Her round face and the softness under her chin. Her expressive mouth and the slight upturn of her freckled nose. Her big, blue eyes that widened when she saw something she liked or when she was surprised. Her gorgeous, bright hair. Her lush bosom and hips, those decadent curves that inspired fantasies of the most impossibly wicked kind in which he worshipped her for hours at a time—

Stop it.

How had it come to this? He had promised himself he would never marry again and here he was, destroying yet another woman by making her his wife.

It was a disaster wholly of his own making. With an unassailable logic, Oliver Hartwell had come to know he had no business touching a woman. But that cold logic had melted like so much spring snow when *she* had touched him, held him, surrounded him with her generous beauty and wished for his happiness.

In her father's study, he had been a knave. He had wanted something, and he had taken it, without a thought for her wants or her well-being.

The next day, he had stood in the Bexton rose garden and watched from afar as her sweetheart berated her. Oliver had been unable to hear exactly what was said but knew the young man's angry words were about what Oliver had done.

In that moment, he had vowed he would always serve those two things first: *her* wants, *her* well-being.

And Nathaniel's. But he had no idea what to do for his son. At least, Henrietta should be able to tell him what she wanted, what she needed. And he would provide that. He must. His selfishness had already deprived her of so much.

His young bride would become his polestar. He would look to her for guidance. He would let her be his example in the years he had left, showing him what to do and how to navigate this misbegotten marriage.

He stood in the hallway just outside the nursery door and listened to her laughter and cajoling and questions and his own son's answering silence. After some minutes, Henrietta's voice subsided, and he could only hear the clicking of the blocks being moved about on the table and Nurse Witherspoon's sighs.

Finally, Henrietta bid Nathaniel and the nurse goodbye, saying she hoped Nathaniel would show her all his toys tomorrow.

She came to the door and looked lost for a moment until she saw him standing there.

"Oh, good." She smiled, but the smile was uncertain. "I thought you had left, and I wouldn't know which way to turn."

He could hear a quaver in her voice. Was she missing her home and her family? She had been quite brave so far, coming to an entirely new place with him as her husband. He knew how he must seem to her—a cold, harsh, forbidding curmudgeon who had buried two wives. An ancient villain who had taken advantage of her sweetness and her innocence. Most girls would be petrified to be married to him. But he shouldn't be surprised Crispin and Georgiana's daughter had pluck.

"Shall I show you to your bedchamber?"

She nodded.

When they went back down the stairs to the warren of bedchambers, he suddenly realized he had no idea which room had been prepared for her. He had some idea she would stay in one of the many rarely-used guest rooms, but he had conveyed no specific request to Mrs. Liddell, his housekeeper.

With a sinking feeling, he surmised Henrietta's trunk had likely been put in the bedchamber next to his. The same one Violet and Emily had occupied, in turn.

He opened the door.

"I'm afraid—" *you will be afraid.*

He cleared his throat and started again. "You may not like this bedchamber and would prefer another. You may have any room you wish."

Henrietta walked in and looked around. "This is lovely." She went to the window. "Oh, the view is perfect. I can see the corner of the stables and off in the distance, I think that's Woldenmere." She turned to him, clasping her hands. "I love the room. Thank you, Oliver."

He must tell her. "You have been put in the bedchamber of the mistress of the house." He nodded at the connecting door. "Our rooms adjoin."

Her face went from smiling to crestfallen, and for a moment he thought her courage had finally failed.

But she said, "Would you prefer I be elsewhere? Maybe you want this room to stay as it is? In memory of your wife? Wives?"

She did not know enough about men to be fearful. He must keep her that way. Protect her always, including from himself.

"No, no," he hastened to assure her. "I only do not want you to be uneasy."

She tilted her head. "I'm not uneasy if you're not uneasy."

He doubted he'd ever rest easy knowing this beauty was sleeping only a few feet away from him, but his own comfort was unimportant.

"If you like the room, it is yours." He could always change bedchambers himself. He'd often thought he should, if only to quell his nightmares. But he deserved the nightmares.

"Good." She broke into another smile just as a late afternoon ray of sunshine came from behind a cloud and forced its way into the room, lighting up her hair like a halo, allowing her ample figure to be seen through her muslin dress. She looked so much like an erotic pagan divinity, he had to mumble an excuse and flee the room like the craven piece of filth he was.

He went to his study and forced himself to read his letters. There weren't many. He had expected to be gone for much longer, to travel all the way to London and spend some weeks there. But he had difficulty attending to what little correspondence had accumulated. His mind kept wandering to Henrietta and the journey they had just taken together.

It had been a trial to spend three days in such close quarters with his new wife's physical charms. And, of course, there had been his own bruising self-reproach about how he had ruined Henrietta's life and done something unforgivable to his only friends, the Staffords.

But there had been delight in that carriage, too. Delight in her company and her questions about the place that would become her home, what he was reading, whether he preferred this, that, or the other. No one, besides Crispin, had ever taken such an interest in him.

Again, he should not be surprised. Like father, like daughter.

She had been uncomplaining and full of good humor even when she had crossed a muddy stable-yard in the rain or when the wine at an inn had been sour with bits of cork floating in it or when they had been far from anywhere and she had asked for the carriage to stop in a woods.

"For what reason?" he enquired, not thinking.

"For a necessary reason," she said. Simple, straightforward, unblushing.

He found it refreshing a young woman would be unembarrassed about her bodily functions. But, still, he should have anticipated, been more solicitous of her needs. He must pay better attention to her.

While also *not* paying attention to her.

He was betwixt the devil and the deep sea.

All of his letters at last read and answered in a somewhat coherent fashion, he did what he always did when he was in his study and had some spare minutes. He went to his table and unrolled his map of the area surrounding Woldenmere, weighing down the corners with his ink pots.

He had left his study door open, but absorbed in looking at his creation, he did not hear Henrietta's approach and was startled by her "Good evening."

He straightened from his bent-over posture. "Good evening."

Her lady's maid and most of her things would not arrive

until the following week, so she must have enlisted a chamber-maid to help her change out of her muslin and into a blue woolen dinner dress. Plain for a duke's daughter, but suitable for a Mrs. Hartwell. Her face was a little flushed and her locks were pinned neatly, but the smallest curls imaginable had formed along the hairline at her forehead and neck. Had she bathed and the steam from the water created those tiny, soft coils? The thought of her voluptuous, bare body in a tub, her skin pink and fragrant, made him tremble.

She came over to where he stood. "What is this?"

He steadied himself by gripping the edge of the table. "A map."

"Oh, I didn't know maps could be so pretty." Her attention was drawn to a place name and she pointed. "Crossthwaite."

"Yes."

Then she saw the pots of different colored inks and the range of quills spread out on the table, and she turned to him, her eyes wide.

Those beautiful eyes. He might drown in them.

"Did you draw this?"

"Yes."

"How long did it take you?"

"It's not yet complete. It takes time to acquire the information. But it gives me an excuse to wander about the district, measuring and sketching."

She turned back to the map. "It's wonderful."

She was sincere. He doubted she could be anything else. A warmth spread over him. Neither Violet nor Emily had ever been interested in his avocation. And he had not known how hungry he was for Henrietta's good opinion.

He offered her his arm, and they went into dinner. He was glad to see she ate well and with pleasure, just as she had at home, just as all the Staffords did.

After the meal, Oliver stood. "In the evenings, I read in the drawing room. You are welcome to join me if you wish. Or you could find your own amusement."

A startled look on her face. She glanced around the dining room and then back to him. "May I take a book from the library?"

He bowed his head. "This is your house."

She found a slender volume quickly, not even looking at the title, and took it to the drawing room and chose a chair by the fire. Oliver sat as well and picked up his newspaper and began to read.

He stole glances at her as he turned pages. She sat, looking at the fire despite the open book on her lap. Still. Serene. A goddess in repose.

He had never seen her father stay still for more than a few minutes. But Henrietta could. So, she had some of her mother's contemplative nature.

After an hour, she bade him good night and went off to bed.

He waited as long as he could. Finally, he went up to his own bedchamber. Hating himself, he put his ear to the connecting door. He heard nothing. She must be asleep.

Goodnight, poor girl.

He was eating his usual breakfast when she came into the dining room in a riding habit, glowing and slightly out of breath.

"Good morning," she chirped as he stood.

He was once more jarred in his expectations. Neither of his wives had ever risen this early. He had heard nothing when he had awoken and pressed his ear again to the connecting door. He had assumed she was still abed.

"I've had the most wonderful morning," she said as she

took her seat. "Thank you, Pearson. Zephyr and I had a really proper gallop. The air, the scenery, all of it is truly glorious."

She had been out and about and ridden already.

Pearson brought her tea and toast. Her eyes darted around the room, at the sideboard, at the toast on Oliver's own plate, before she took her toast in hand, spread a good coat of jam atop it, and began to eat.

Only after he had left the breakfast table to go to the stables himself, did he reflect that toast and jam and tea was not an adequate breakfast for a healthy young woman who must have ridden for miles this morning.

He turned around and made his way to the kitchen.

"Mrs. Nixon, tomorrow and all the days going forward, I would like a full breakfast to be prepared. Hot food and plenty of it." Like what was served at Bexton Manor. "You must consult Mrs. Hartwell on menus, of course. And be sure to give her a substantial luncheon today."

"Yes, Mr. Hartwell."

The rest of his day was spent checking on his land, his sheep, his shepherds, his tenants, just as he did after any time away.

When he came back to Crossthwaite, he stabled his horse and walked through the kitchen garden to go back into the house. Unlike Bexton Manor, there were no opulent flower beds here. He was too practical, Violet had had no interest, and Emily had been too weak to even contemplate such an undertaking.

And Emily had said she adored flowers. He should have seen to some plantings if only for the pleasure it might have given her to know something was growing while she lay in her bed, giving all her strength to the son growing inside her. Another failure on his part, but one he would not make again.

He came upon his new wife and his son, both squatting

next to a row of cabbages, their attention on the ground in front of them. Silent.

Neither looked up until his shadow fell over them. Then Henrietta raised her head, but his son kept looking at the ground.

"Good afternoon, Oliver," she said. He liked how she lilted his name, how she greeted him with a grin. "We are busy watching a caterpillar make his way."

He hitched the knees of his trousers up a bit and crouched down to join them. The green-purple worm they were observing was an ugly creature he would have dismissed out of hand as a pest.

"I was just saying this is a puss moth." She pointed. "See? It has a saddle. When I was your age, Nathaniel, I thought this kind of caterpillar might be a good mount for a faery."

Nathaniel looked up at her, his eyes wide.

"What do you think?" she asked the boy. "Do you like this one better than the knot grass caterpillar? With the fuzz and red dots?"

A quick nod of his son's head and then he turned his dark eyes on Oliver.

Oliver cleared his throat. "I like this one better, too." He couldn't recall ever looking at a caterpillar in his life.

Nathaniel's eyes went back down to the caterpillar. For long minutes, all three of them watched the little animal inch along, and Oliver felt something strange and unexpected.

Peace.

Later, he was pleased to see the dinner table boasted more dishes than it had the night before, and Henrietta again ate well.

But she asked about Nathaniel. When he had first walked, first spoken. What he liked to do. Where and when and how he took his meals. And what did the doctor say about his health?

Oliver was embarrassed how little he knew about his son. Distress crept over him. He didn't need this girl-wife to point out what an inadequate father he was. He knew it already.

He was vastly relieved when the meal was over. He stood, and she looked up.

"Oh, won't you have pudding?"

Her expression was distraught, her voice pleading, her strong emotion incongruous with the subject matter of her request.

He sat. If it was important to her, it was important to him.

"I will stay while you eat your pudding."

"You won't have any?"

"A small portion," he told Pearson.

He didn't even look at what was put in front of him. Out of a desire to please his new wife, he took a bite of something he didn't want. But as the rich creaminess spread across his tongue, he looked at the plate.

This was a custard of the same ilk he was always served at Bexton Manor.

Exactly the same.

Henrietta must have gotten the receipt from the Bexton Manor cook and given it to Mrs. Nixon.

"This is very good," he said, clicking his spoon against the plate. He turned to Pearson. "I'll have another bit, I think. A big bit."

He couldn't help but notice Henrietta watching him eat every spoonful.

"Tell me, Henrietta." He paused. It was the first time he had ever addressed her without the attached *Lady*, and he saw her take note of it. A small swallow, a bit more pink in her cheeks. "Tell me, do you like flowers?"

NINE

OCTOBER. 1817.

In only a month, Crossthwaite had changed.

Oliver no longer ate alone, unless he chose to. But he never chose to, even coming back to the house at midday to join Henrietta for luncheon, a meal he had never made a habit of eating before.

There was more noise about the house now. Henrietta gaily talking to the servants, running up and down the stairs, humming to herself as she tended to some task, coaxing Nathaniel into a game or a song or a walk.

And, every few days, there was custard.

Henrietta gave up the pretense of reading in the evenings. Instead, she plied her needle. He saw her squinting, trying to angle her hoop towards the fire. He got up and moved a small table to one of her elbows and lit and placed an additional lamp.

"Oh, thank you," she said, looking up at him with shining eyes and a wide smile, far too grateful for something that had only taken him a few moments. He must do more for her.

"You have given up reading," he observed as he took his seat again.

"I've never been much of a reader, but I wanted to sit with you, so I made do with a book. But Lucy brought my embroidery with the rest of my things, so I have it now."

She *wanted* to sit with him. She wanted to sit with *him*. He ignored the knot that had just tied itself around his heart and squeezed. Instead, he said stiffly, "You must always tell me if there is something you want or need."

"Oh. Yes. But I have it now." She flourished her hoop at him. "I hope you don't think it silly."

"Silly?"

She blushed. "Gentlemen sometimes think feminine pursuits foolish."

"I'll remind you that I'm a farmer who draws maps."

"Oh, but maps are meant to be useful, aren't they?"

"Mine aren't."

"What are they for?"

There was only one answer for that. "Me."

They gazed at each other. Finally, she bent her head again to her stitching, and he went back behind his newspaper.

Minutes later, he heard her murmur, "I'm glad you have something for yourself."

An afternoon came when he stayed home because it had begun to rain during luncheon. He retired to his study, meaning to work on his map, but the house was too quiet, and he didn't like it. He had become used to a bit of hubbub.

No. It wasn't the quiet that was bothering him. He craved *her*. Not in the carnal way he usually did. He just wanted to see her. Hear her. Smell her. Something.

He went in search of his wife and found her in the nursery. The curtains had been drawn and the room was dark, but he could make her out, kneeling by the side of Nathaniel's low bed.

"Close your eyes," she crooned. "If you close your eyes, I'll tell you a story."

"Caterpillar?" his son asked.

"Yes, one about a caterpillar."

Her hand moved and did something. Was she stroking Nathaniel's forehead?

"You have a curl here when it rains. Like your father."

"Caterpillar," Nathaniel demanded.

A soft laugh from her. "You haven't closed your eyes yet."

His son must then have closed his eyes.

"Once there was a green caterpillar who lived in the garden. His name was Crawley."

"Crawley." Was that a note of amusement in his son's voice?

"Keep your eyes closed," she said and there was a pause before her melodious, soothing voice went on. "He liked to crawl. He liked to creep. He was very good at doing both things. But his favorite thing was to find a thick stem of a nice, sturdy plant. And then he would climb. He would climb and climb and climb and climb…"

As she went on, talking about the climbing caterpillar and the broad, green leaves he would take shelter under when it rained, Oliver thought his own eyes might close. Finally, she stopped speaking. He waited, thinking she would get up now, leave the room and join him in the hallway, let Nathaniel sleep.

But she didn't. She stayed by the side of the bed, her hand moving slowly, stroking Nathaniel's forehead.

What would it be like to go to sleep to Henrietta's voice and her hand stroking his forehead? Oh, how he envied his son.

She turned her head towards the door and whispered, "I promised Nathaniel I'd stay while he slept."

So, she knew Oliver was there.

He retreated quietly down the hallway and the stairs and went to his own bedchamber to seek out a looking glass. Did he really have a curl on his forehead when it rained? Yes, indeed, the mirror revealed a dangling lock. He pushed the hair back, but a moment later, it fell down again. Perhaps some pomade could fix it in place or he should have his hair cut shorter.

But did Henrietta like the curl? As a rule, she seemed far more concerned with cleanliness than tidiness, and in the course of a day, a few of her own curls would often fly loose from her pins. And he liked to see her that way, her hair a bit mussed. As unguarded with her appearance as she was with everything else.

Perhaps, then, she also liked his curl.

He wouldn't have his hair cut or buy any pomade. Just yet.

TEN

December. 1817.

Oliver was long past due for a trip to London.

His journeys had been needlessly frequent before, motivated by the desire to have an excuse to spend time at Bexton Manor on the way there and back.

But now, well, he was not sure of his welcome with the Staffords. He and Crispin had resumed their usual correspondence, but things might be different in person. And even if the duke and duchess exhibited perfect cordiality towards their new son-in-law, Oliver knew himself. His remorse would create a distance where there had been none, introduce an awkwardness where all had been ease before.

And for the first time in years, he had no desire to leave Crossthwaite. It was a pity to have to tear himself away just now when there was such bustling hope and lightheartedness all around him, when he had a piece of Bexton Manor in his own house. But his inherited business concerns had pressing matters requiring his presence in London.

On the morning he planned to set out, he gazed over the rim of his teacup at Henrietta. She was picking at her food, stealing glances at him but then looking away when he met her eyes. She was dressed for riding but apparently had not yet taken her giant gelding out this morning.

Could this delay in her usual exercise mean she had not wanted to risk missing his departure? Oh, no. Was she going to inflict some maudlin leave-taking on her husband-in-name?

He couldn't allow that. He wouldn't survive it.

Oliver stood abruptly. She started to stand, too, but he stayed her with a gesture of his hand.

"There's no need to neglect your breakfast. I will say my farewells here. I will be back before the new year."

She nodded and kept her seat. Good, he would be spared. And her eyes were dry. He had been a fool to think she would display emotion at his leaving. It wasn't as if she had married him by choice or she had any true attachment to him.

But as he went to exit the room, she cried "Oliver!" and threw herself out of her chair and hugged him, just as she had in her father's study. This time, she wrapped her arms around his neck instead of his sides, leaving his arms free to embrace her in return. Unbidden, his arms came up and went around her as she pressed into him.

Their first embrace since that fateful one. The kiss—that unconscionable, ruinous kiss—came into his mind. A tender moment suddenly turned into something dark and guilty, stained by his own depravity. He stepped away from her, taking her arms from his neck, averting his eyes.

"Did you put the list of things you want from London in my satchel?" he asked, trying to inject something proper and pragmatic into this exchange.

"Yes," she said, and he could hear the tears in her voice.

He nodded and left the room without looking at or speaking to her again. He couldn't.

In front of the house, he supervised the loading of his trunk and discussed the first part of the journey with his coachman. As he was about to get into the carriage, he heard, "Wait, wait, wait! Oliver!"

Henrietta flew out the door, holding his son in her arms.

"Nathaniel did not get a chance to say goodbye to you," she gasped, her warm breath making white puffs in the chilly air.

Oliver had never bid farewell to his own son before. He had always been too apprehensive. Irrationally fearful. He had not wanted the sickly boy to receive a goodbye from his father when there was a very real chance it might be a final adieu and Nathaniel would succumb to an illness while Oliver was away.

But Nathaniel did not look sickly right now. He hadn't looked sickly in weeks. His cheeks were pink and slightly rounded and his arms were fiercely clinging to his stepmother's neck.

"Do you want to hug your father goodbye?" Henrietta asked him.

Nathaniel just held on tighter to her and turned his head away from Oliver.

"It's all right," Oliver said. But he could tell Henrietta was distressed. "We could shake hands like men do," he offered.

"Yes." Henrietta sounded relieved. "Nathaniel, please do shake hands with your father."

The boy looked first at Henrietta and then tilted his head to look at Oliver out of the corner of his eye. After several seconds consideration, he thrust out his hand. Oliver took it and gravely shook it.

"Nicely done, darling," Henrietta breathed.

Oliver let himself, for a moment, imagine the *darling* was for him.

He got into the carriage and when it turned at the end of the drive and he dared look back, he saw Henrietta still standing out in the cold, Nathaniel held on her hip, her other arm above her head, sweeping back and forth in large arcs like she was a castaway hailing a passing ship.

Over the next three weeks, a waking hour did not go by in which he didn't conjure the feel of her body against his, the sound of his name on her lips, the sight of her holding his son and waving farewell to him.

These reveries made him hurry through his meetings surrounding the shipping interests and the brewery left to him by his deceased father. The unexpected expiry of Mr. Oliver Hartwell's ataraxy likely provoked some head-scratching among his solicitors and men of business. He was impatient, short-tempered, demanding. Issues must be resolved immediately, and the new contracts written out and signed without delay. He could not linger. The new year was much too distant. He must be back at Crossthwaite by Christmas Day.

On the morning of his last day in London, he finally took out Henrietta's list. He had held the shopping back as a treat for himself, looking forward to spending uninterrupted hours thinking of her, searching out and procuring things she wanted for herself. He expected the list to include some bolts of cloth to be made into dresses at a future time. Would she describe exactly what she wanted, or would she leave the color and pattern of the fabric to his taste? Would she want some luxurious, scented soap or expensive perfume? Ribbons or threads for her embroidery? Would she allow him the latitude to select a bonnet for her? Might a husband be allowed to purchase stockings for his wife?

But when he unfolded the list, he found:

1. *Top, brightly colored. Red or yellow?*
2. *Ball, a good sized one, for you and N. to throw about and kick.*
3. *Bilbocatch.*
4. *Hobbyhorse, if not too dear.*

   5. *Shuttlecock/Battledores.*
   6. *Books (simple) about insects, butterflies, spiders, worms, &c (with illustrated plates, please) for you to read to N. (again, if not too dear).*

His hand swept over the foolscap, smoothing it, over and over. For an hour, he sat and smoothed the piece of paper. He considered the list. He considered his son. He considered his own miserable and half-hearted efforts at paternity. And, most of all, he considered Henrietta, his polestar, and how she was showing him the path forward in the kindest way possible.

The path of play.

Finally, he folded the page, tucked it into the tailcoat pocket closest to his heart, and set out, determined to get everything on the list and a few more things, besides.

When he disembarked in front of Crossthwaite on Christmas Eve, his legs stiff and creaking from too many days in his carriage without respite, the front door banged open and Henrietta ran out.

He was ready for her. He held his arms open and she ran into them.

"You're home! Welcome home, Oliver," she said into his chest.

He bent his head down and smelled her hair. Juniper and burnt sugar.

"Happy Christmas, Henrietta," he said, his voice choking only a little on her name. In that moment, he decided he would sell the London businesses. He didn't want them. He didn't need them. And he never wanted to travel away from here again.

Far too soon, she was releasing him, turning towards the house and crouching down.

"Come down, too," she whispered, tugging on his hand.

Mystified, he crouched with her, not wanting to release her hand.

Nathaniel, looking impossibly well and surely half a stone heavier in weight and an inch taller in height, came out the front door now, almost as fast as Henrietta had, bolting right towards his father.

Then and there, Oliver received his very first hug, ever, from his son. It lasted only a second, if that—Nathaniel's slender arms around Oliver's neck, warm cheek against his cold one, his own hand coming up to touch his son's narrow back, so like his own—before Nathaniel squirmed away.

Thank God, the embrace had been short and Oliver could stand and busy himself with removing parcels from the carriage. He was almost completely recovered when he turned back to Henrietta who took his arm, hugging it against herself and her breasts as she led him into the house, burbling about Christmas and the greenery she and Nathaniel had collected and Mrs. Nixon's ginger cake in the oven and could he smell it?

It was the finest homecoming a man could ask for and a far better one than he deserved.

ELEVEN
April. 1818.

Henrietta had been married for almost eight months now. Two-thirds of a year.

She had learned many things about her husband in that time. He was widely considered to be a diligent and fair man, kind to his workers and helpful to his tenants. He read a newspaper in the evening after dinner. He still liked Mrs. Blaire's custard, even though Henrietta was the one cooking it now. He was making a map of the Lake District, and not a dull, dry one, but a charming one, full of all kinds of cunning little drawings.

He always smelled good to her, even when his work had involved some hard labor that day and he had just come into the house, greeting her on the stairs, brushing by her on his way to his wash. He might have had to deal with some farming unpleasantness, but there was some essential rightness to his own smell that overcame any stench.

Oh, and he had beautiful hands and wrists and arms. She had spent many hours observing his hands—his long palms topped by his strong yet elegant fingers, holding his newspaper, wielding his knife and fork—but only last month, she had gotten her first look at his forearms.

She had decided to take Nathaniel out in the dog cart to observe the sheep shearing. All the men had taken off their coats and rolled up their sleeves, but it was Oliver's forearms that had heated her body and made a trickle of sweat course between her breasts on the cold March morning.

That span from Oliver's elbow to his hand was long, of course, like all the rest of him, but also ropy with muscle and sinew and branching veins when he lifted a ewe. A sparse mat of dark hair on the outside and golden skin on the inside.

Henrietta didn't think it was wifely to pine, but she let herself shed a few tears of longing for those forearms when she was alone in her bed that night.

But the most important thing she had learned about her husband was that he loved his son. He did. Somehow, sometime in the past, Oliver had let himself get all foolishly twisted up in his thoughts and actions and emotions. In the midst of pushing away those big feelings he thought he could not tolerate, he'd also pushed away his son. Henrietta didn't know why Oliver had believed he wasn't strong enough before, but now he had found the belief or the strength from somewhere.

Because much of what had been wrong between father and son had come right in the last several months.

This winter, Oliver had devoted time and care and attention to Nathaniel. The two had played together and read together and even occasionally napped together on a sofa in the drawing room, Nathaniel's dark head tucked into his father's chest as Oliver's arm curled around his son protectively.

There was nothing that made her happier than witnessing that growing closeness.

Except, perhaps, if something similar might happen between herself and Oliver?

He was unfailingly kind to her. He trusted her with everything in the house, despite her youth and inexperience. He had allowed her to take charge of Nathaniel's food, his sleep, his simple lessons.

And he had, unexpectedly, given her the most marvelous, romantic Christmas gifts, ones that hinted at an intimacy between them that did not exist.

Rose-scented perfume. A reference to where they had become betrothed?

Yards of blue muslin in the exact shade of her eyes.

A bolt of pink taffeta. The month before Christmas, she had mentioned she loved pink, but never wore the color because a London modiste had told her she couldn't. The redness of her hair was to blame. And when she had torn the wrappings from the bolt on Christmas morning, Oliver had said stiffly, "You should wear what pleases you. And I think you would look very well in any color."

And silk stockings. Silk stockings! From a man who had never seen her legs, let alone touched them.

He tolerated her affection—her hand grabbing his, her hugs, her kisses atop his head when he was seated or on his cheek when he was standing and she went up on her toes. She bestowed all the same caresses on him that she gave to Nathaniel or she would give to members of her family.

But he never reached for her.

Never.

She had never spoken to anyone, not even her mother, about her secret shame. That her husband did not want her in his bed.

Oliver never spoke of his previous wives, so she knew almost nothing about them beyond the painting of the beautiful, fragile Emily. Henrietta never allowed gossip to be repeated in front of her, so when her lady's maid had tried to tell her some of the below-stairs talk, Henrietta had hushed her immediately, saying, "If my husband wants me to know something, he'll tell me himself, Lucy."

She had dared to ask Oliver one or two questions about her predecessors, but she could see with her own eyes he didn't like to talk of the past and his losses, so she stopped asking. After all, she was trying to make him happy, not sad. Much better to tell him how Nathaniel had learned his numbers up to one hundred because he wanted to draw a centipede or to laugh over Oliver's stories about the one wily ram who always left his fellow rams to invade the ewes' pasture or to repeat the family news contained in her most recent letter from Bexton Manor.

She also stopped asking questions about the previous Mrs. Hartwells because, as the months went by, she discovered certain things about herself.

First, she was a coward and didn't want to hear about the women Oliver had chosen. Women he had married of his own volition and lain with.

Second, she was a horribly jealous, petty thing.

Third, she was in love with her husband, and she wished desperately, more than anything, that he would be in love with her, too.

TWELVE
AUGUST. 1818.

"Y ou needn't, you know," he said on the eve of her twentieth birthday and Nathaniel's fourth birthday. There had been a silence between them for a good half an hour, during which he had been hiding behind his newspaper and steeling himself to say this to her.

"Needn't what?" She looked up from her embroidery.

"Stay here."

He had seen no evidence she wanted to leave. She had said nothing, done nothing to suggest that. On the contrary, she had woven herself into the fabric of Crossthwaite and the village beyond in a way he himself hadn't in his over twenty years of owning the property. She had met every occupant of Woldenmere and knew every granny, every child, every dog, probably every chicken and cow.

But he would not make the same mistake he had made with Violet. Henrietta needed to know she was not bound to him and she could have another life, one of her own choosing. Hadn't he vowed to put her needs always above his own? He must keep that vow. No matter the pain it would cause him. No matter he no longer could fathom a life without her.

No matter that both his and Nathaniel's hearts would break should she leave.

"I'll buy or rent a house for you, anywhere you like, give you ample money for a household. Nothing as grand as Bexton Manor, of course, but something suitable."

She blinked and her head bent again to her stitchery and all he could see were her sunset curls, her nimble fingers poking the needle in and out.

When she spoke, her voice was low. "Do you want me to go?"

"No!" The word burst from him with a greater force than he intended. "No, but I want you to be happy."

She continued to keep her eyes down, to stitch. "I'm happy. Are you happy?"

What was his answer to be? As long as she didn't leave, it was a resounding, heartfelt *yes*. But he didn't know how to be heartfelt, so he merely uttered the word.

"Yes."

She finally lifted her head. Were those tears in her eyes?

"Oh, I'm so relieved and glad, Oliver. I don't want to leave. I love," she almost choked, "Crossthwaite."

He wanted to be sure, and he wanted to know how to keep her happy in his home. "You're not bored? Lonely?"

"How could I be bored or lonely? There's so much to keep me occupied. The house, the village, the countryside, Nathaniel, Zephyr. I'm busy as a bee."

He felt a small pang that he was not on the list of things that kept her from being lonely at Crossthwaite.

"You needn't bother yourself about the house. Mrs. Liddell did an adequate job on her own before you came. "

"I like being mistress of the house."

He raised his eyebrows. "A duke's daughter shouldn't be doing laundry."

She laughed. "I don't do laundry. Not really. Not the hard

parts, the soaking and the scrubbing and the wringing. I just do the hanging up and taking down. And folding it and putting it away. I like that."

"As long as you like it."

"I do."

"And," he said carefully, "you needn't make custard. You could tell Mrs. Nixon how to make it."

Her face colored and she dropped her embroidery hoop into her lap and twisted her hands together. "You know?"

"Word got back to me."

"But I like making custard, too."

"Good. Because I like eating your custard."

He couldn't help but lay a subtle emphasis on *your*. Since he had found out she was the one who made the custard, he thought it even more delicious. When he ate it, he felt he was filling himself up with her. Her care. Her sweetness.

"Good." She smiled. "I'm glad you know my secret." She picked up her embroidery hoop and her smile turned a bit mischievous. "And I'll tell you another one. Because I wasn't perfectly truthful with you, just now."

Apprehension threw tight, iron bands around his chest and compressed the air out of his lungs. He had been so sure the custard-making was her only secret. And it was such a silly, harmless one. What painful truth was she about to reveal?

"I do have a little bit of time on my hands occasionally, and there's something I'd like to do with it."

Go to Paris? Take up with a lover?

"I'd like to learn saddlery."

He shook his head, not understanding.

"I want to learn how to make a saddle."

He was still bewildered. "You want to learn a trade?"

"No. I just…I've had an idea for a while. For a special saddle for myself and Zephyr. And I'd like to be the one to make it. If you would take me to Lancaster, I can have a tree made there for my saddle and I could buy the tools and leather I need. I was thinking Mr. Spedding might be willing to give me some lessons in how to cut and stitch the leather? And I could use the extra harness room in our stables to do my work."

Our stables. She had said *our*. She wasn't going anywhere. The strain and weight of the invisible iron bands dropped away, and he felt like a boy.

All things were possible once again.

He took up his newspaper, hoping to give an appearance of nonchalance rather than ecstasy. "I'm going into the village tomorrow. Shall I have a word with Mr. Spedding about the lessons?"

She beamed. "Oh, yes, would you? If you ask, he'll be sure to say yes."

Oliver was fairly certain Spedding would be far more likely to say yes if the pretty, young Mrs. Hartwell asked him herself, but Oliver would hammer out a fee for the lessons, make certain there was nothing dangerous for Henrietta in the undertaking. No chance of lopped-off fingers, for example.

And he'd make sure Spedding didn't have any strapping, young apprentices about. Ones with flirtatious ways and wandering, greedy hands. Henrietta had no idea of her effect on men. And still no idea some men were depraved animals.

Like me.

He straightened a page of the newspaper. "Would next week suit for going to Lancaster?"

"Oh, Oliver!"

A flurry of skirts as Henrietta jumped up and suddenly she was in front of him, almost in his lap, leaning over, pressing into him, hugging him from a standing position as he sat, her breasts nudging under his chin.

Time had not made her touch any less arousing for him. He didn't know how it was possible, but each time she came near him, his physical desire for her grew incrementally. At this point, a quick kiss on his cheek accompanied by an unintentional graze of her bosom against his arm could keep him awake all night, painfully hard until he capitulated and used his hand while thinking of the softness of her lips and breasts.

"Thank you, thank you, thank you, Oliver!"

He allowed himself to take one hand off the crumpled newspaper in his lap and pat her back lightly, tentatively.

"You're welcome." He swallowed, committing this embrace to his memory, adding it to his catalogue of her caresses. "Henrietta."

She pulled back slightly, her eyes enormous with delight, her arms still resting on his shoulders. "You're the dearest husband in the whole world."

"At Crossthwaite, certainly," he said and raised his eyebrows. Her puffery embarrassed him, especially when he knew he wasn't anything like a real husband to her.

But she didn't smile or laugh at his deflection. She just shook her head.

"Oliver Hartwell, when are you going to realize Crossthwaite *is* the whole world to me?"

A moment came and went when he could have leaned forward and kissed her lips. But it was not for him to do that. He had done that once and ruined her life.

Her eyes dropped to his mouth, and he felt a throb in his cock at the thought that she might kiss him.

Kiss me, he willed her. *I could live happily, forever, on just one more kiss. Kiss me.*

She did not. She withdrew her arms and went back to her chair, settling to her embroidery in a most industrious manner, avoiding his eyes.

Would she ever feel anything for him beyond companionship?

No. He was too old, and even when young, he had not

been a man who inspired passion in women. Certainly not in a beautiful woman like Henrietta who should have married a prince or an heir to a dukedom or, at the very least, a man closer to her own age. A happy man. One without his scars. One who knew how to give and receive love.

He must remember Henrietta was just a remarkably caring and affectionate person and as her husband, he was lucky enough to receive some of that care and affection. That was all.

Why then did he still long for more?

From the grave, a wrathful Violet answered him.

Because you're a filthy beast, Oliver Hartwell.

THIRTEEN

JUNE. 1819.

One fine summer morning, Oliver took a jaunt. Every month or so, he would set out with his drawing tools, his viameter, and explore a new patch of land, taking notes and sketching in preparation for adding the area to his map.

To his great joy, Henrietta had come along several times, and now she asked if Nathaniel could come, as well.

"I'll keep Nathaniel diverted, so you can do your work," she assured him.

It wasn't work for Oliver, but he liked that she thought of his map making as a serious undertaking.

All three of them rode out in the brake with several large baskets packed into the back. Nathaniel sat between his father and Henrietta, occasionally bouncing with excitement.

Once at the chosen spot, Oliver walked and measured and sketched the view from the high meadow while Henrietta and Nathaniel played with the shuttlecock and battledores, even at times using one of the ancient dry stone walls as a separation between them to bat the shuttlecock back and forth.

After a while, Nathaniel asked Henrietta for the butterfly

net she had fashioned for him. He leapt and ran and swooped the net with precision and caught butterfly after butterfly with astonishing ease. All of which he let go.

The day had started off cloudless, but suddenly the sun dimmed and a light rain began to fall. Henrietta laughed when a particularly large drop hit her nose with a splash, but Nathaniel scowled, saying he couldn't catch butterflies in the rain.

"Let's have our picnic under that tree, then," Henrietta said, picking up the baskets.

"I have a better idea," Oliver said.

The horse had been unharnessed from the brake and was tethered to the ground nearby, grazing, undisturbed by the rain. Oliver got on his hands and knees and went under the brake and spread the picnic blanket on the dry grass there.

"Come under here." He poked his head out and was rewarded by a giggle from his son who must have thought it funny to see his father under the wagon.

Nathaniel and Henrietta both crawled under the brake and after some arranging and Oliver making sure no limbs were in the way of a wheel in case the wedges failed to stop the brake from rolling, they were comfortable. Snug and dry.

Nathaniel and perhaps even Henrietta might have been able to sit upright under the brake, but since Oliver couldn't, they joined him in lying down for their picnic.

"Like the ancient Romans," Oliver said and then had to explain to Nathaniel how the Romans had eaten lying down.

After a bit, with the soothing patter of the rain, a stomach full of cheese sandwiches, and the exertion of the morning, Nathaniel fell asleep in the middle of the blanket.

Oliver was on his side, resting his head on his hand, and Henrietta had taken the same position. Their faces were only a few feet apart. It had not seemed dangerously intimate until Nathaniel had fallen asleep. But now it did.

Oliver touched the back of Nathaniel's dark head lightly. "You didn't have to tell the caterpillar story to get him to nod off."

"Running about was enough."

"My son, the lepidopterist."

"What is that?"

"A person who collects butterflies. Studies them."

"What is the word for a person who makes maps?"

"A mapmaker. But you're right. There should be a fancy word like lepidopterist. Chorographer. Chartographer. Cartographer."

She laughed. "That's you. You're a cartographer."

"No, not really. But I thought I might be." He rolled onto his back and looked at the underside of the brake rather than at Henrietta.

"Once upon a time," he started and then stopped.

"All the best stories begin that way," she said encouragingly.

"When I was young, I wanted to be an explorer, see new lands, discover things."

He cast a glance at her. He felt it was a laughable ambition now when his life was so confined, so timid. But she did not laugh. Her face was still. She was listening. He shifted his eyes back, away from her.

"So, after I left Eton, I did not go to university or go to work for my father's businesses. Instead, I joined an expedition to the East Indies."

He had quickly made a discovery on that voyage, but not of an uncharted island or a hidden reef. No, he had discovered Oliver Hartwell could not tolerate life on board a ship. Not one whit. And his wretched vomiting never subsided, even after weeks at sea. Fearing Oliver might die, the captain finally put him ashore at Cape Town, so Oliver might build up enough strength for the dreaded return trip to England by a different ship. He made it back to Portsmouth barely alive, according to the ship's doctor. He had been skeletal and wasted, skin collapsed, his mouth a desert of sores.

Oliver Hartwell was doomed never to leave the island of Britain again.

Henrietta's voice was full of enthusiasm and excitement. "You've been to the East Indies? That's marvelous! How could I not know that?"

"Because I haven't. I never went. Incurable seasickness. I had to quit the idea of a life of adventuring."

The sound of the rain hitting the topside of the brake filled the hush that followed.

"How terrible. How terrible that must have been for you."

No one had ever truly sympathized with him over the loss of his boyhood dreams. Even Crispin had never understood how deep the wound had gone. How, after that, it had taken all of Oliver's strength, physically and mentally, to go back out into the world and try to find something that interested him.

"Were you crushed, Oliver?"

He turned towards her, on his side again, and looked at her face. Those blue eyes were welling, her bottom lip was trembling. For him. For that long-ago Oliver Hartwell, the boy-man he had been at her age.

"I was. But I still liked maps. And that was when I chanced on your father again, having not seen him for six years."

"Papa always said you're the reason he got Mama to marry him," she said, brushing at her eyes. "You helped him woo her."

"He did all the wooing. I just showed him the back entrance to the British Museum Reading Room. But we became friends after that."

She smiled through her tears. "I'm glad you had a friend. I'm glad it was my father."

"He was the one who helped me decide what to do with my life. He asked me questions about what I liked. What I wanted."

What he had wanted, initially, had been what Crispin had found for himself. A wife. But Oliver was still too young, too unsure of himself, too untested. First, he must settle to a living. And Crispin helped him see how natural beauty and a life connected to the out-of-doors and the seasons would improve his health and lift his spirits.

After long hours mulling it over, Oliver decided if he must be consigned to a landlocked life in England, he should be in the prettiest part of it. He studied landscape paintings, pored over maps, and decided on the Lake District.

He sold half of his deceased father's business interests—the ones that could not be managed from afar—and bought Crossthwaite and became a yeoman farmer. He succeeded at his agricultural pursuits and bought more land and put sheep on the pasture, rented some to tenants. He had time to climb fells and swim in meres and read. But a wife still eluded him.

Finally, Crispin and Georgiana took him in hand, insisted he attend their dinner parties when he visited them in London. That was where Oliver had met Violet Winter.

But he could not speak of Violet. Especially not to Henrietta, even though he was sure she must already know the sordid story from the villagers or the Crossthwaite servants or her own parents. He must move the conversation away from himself and his poisonous past.

He could feel the curl dangling, brushing his forehead, but he did not push it back.

"What do you like, Henrietta?" he asked her. "What do you want?"

"You know what I like, and you give me everything I want. Even before I ask for it, sometimes."

He meant large things. Intangible things. Hopes and dreams. Not silk threads or a packet of saffron.

But she must have known that. She called herself slow, but she wasn't. She understood what he had asked her.

Henrietta rolled onto her stomach and rested her cheek on her folded hands in front of her, her elbows akimbo, her face turned away from him, hidden.

Whatever his wife dreamed of, she could not bring herself to tell him.

The rain pitter-pattered on and off for another hour, and Oliver spent that time trying not to look at the curves of Henrietta's bottom, perfectly outlined by the clinging drapery of her summer dress.

She did not move until Nathaniel awoke and asked for another biscuit. Then she turned her head and blinked her eyes and smiled and seemed herself even when the rain stopped and they headed back to Crossthwaite.

Oliver Hartwell thought he knew his wife. But, maybe, he didn't, at all.

Part Three

Bed Me, Husband

FOURTEEN

Henrietta buried her nose in the tall stack of Oliver's folded shirts. Although she adored the scent of his shirts before laundering, the smell of clean linen was its own, if lesser, pleasure. She managed to get a hand on the door knob without letting the stack slip and used her hip to bump the bedchamber door open the rest of the way.

But Oliver was not in his study as she had thought he was.

Oliver was in his bedchamber, dressed as she had seen him last, sitting on the edge of his bed, holding himself.

Touching himself.

She noticed out of the corner of her eye that his head moved—perhaps to look at her coming into the room—but she found it impossible to take her attention off the organ in his hand.

How did his phallus fit into his trousers? It was so large and thick, poking out quite a far distance from a nest of black hair. And it was a dark and angry red, an entirely different color from the rest of his golden skin. And his hand was moving so quickly, so forcefully. Wouldn't he hurt himself?

It seemed like forever, but it was likely only a second or

two before she heard a choking sound and white material fountained out of him. Seed. So much seed. His other hand was right there in his lap, holding a handkerchief. He must have intended to catch his seed and forgotten.

"Henrietta." The word was a harsh rasp. She finally looked away from his phallus, and, oh, she had never seen such a rueful look as that upon the face of her husband.

"Your shirts," she got out and put the stack down on a chair and fled into her own chamber. She locked both doors and threw herself down onto her bed, her whole body aflame, consumed by such a rush of need that she could not even stand.

She had finally seen the man she loved, the man she desired, undone by his own desire.

She clawed at her skirts in a frenzy. She was damp, her nub already swollen, and she rubbed herself with the same fierceness Oliver had used on himself. Indeed, in her mind, he had his long fingers on her, demanding her climax.

Within a minute, she was gasping out her release as waves of rapture rocked her body.

Relief. Followed by tears.

Because as pleasure ebbed away, an enormous loneliness rushed in like a terrible tide.

Poor her. And poor Oliver. He tended to himself when she'd be so happy to tend to him. More than happy. But he didn't want that. He had warned her before they married he didn't want that.

What had he said? He would not impose on her.

She wiped her tears on her sleeve. They had been married for two years. Knowing her feelings now, her want, her need, would she still marry Oliver?

Yes.

Yes, of course, she would still marry Oliver. She didn't want a life without him, without Nathaniel. She didn't have what her parents had, but look at how much she *did* have. So many people didn't have love. Better to have love without copulation than the other way around.

Because there was an abundance of love here at Crossthwaite. Her love for Oliver and Nathaniel. Nathaniel's love for both her and Oliver. Oliver's for Nathaniel.

And Oliver was fond of her. He didn't love her the way he must have loved his previous wives, but she knew he cared for her. He was so thoughtful, so obliging, he always said she could have anything she wanted—

Wait.

Did he know she wanted him? That she had nursed thoughts of him for years, even before they married? That, in her imagination, he had been present each and every time she had ever achieved ecstasy?

Please, God, no. Please don't let him know. I couldn't bear his knowing how much I've yearned for him. How much I still do.

But this was a foolish worry. He couldn't know. No one knew. Henrietta had been so careful to limit herself to friendly hugs, kisses on the cheek, brief touches. She'd denied herself so many times. Painfully many times. There was no way he could know.

But.

If she decided to make her desire known to him, would he fornicate with her just because she wanted him? Would he give himself to her, just as he had given her everything else she had ever asked for? Like the saddle-making lessons and embroidery needles and even things she hadn't asked for, like silk stockings and perfume?

She toyed with the idea. Asking for *that*. With her husband. Who did not return her desire.

No. She couldn't. She had longings at times that threatened to overwhelm her, but she couldn't bear telling him she wanted him when he didn't want her.

She didn't even know how she would face him at dinner tonight. Knowing he knew she knew he took his pleasure alone. Rather than with her.

She would just have to pretend like this afternoon had never happened.

Oliver must have made the same decision because that evening they looked at each other over the dining table and spoke without awkwardness about all the usual, ordinary things—the celebration of her and Nathaniel's birthday in two days, the house, the sheep, the shepherds, the tenants, happenings in the village. And after dinner, as usual, he read his newspaper, and she embroidered.

But, in bed that night, she thought of Oliver lying alone in his own bed and what he had said two years ago on the eve of their wedding.

He would not impose on her. She had no obligation to him; all the obligation was on his side. She did not need to fear his coming into her bed.

At the time, she had felt sure she knew the reason why he didn't want to perform his marital duty. He wasn't attracted to her, just like so many of the young lords during her Season. Just like Geoffrey.

And although he had been very polite when he told her their marriage would be a chaste one, she had been hurt. But she had never been one to linger on unhappiness or to hold grievances. It was better to keep going and to concentrate on more joyous things.

But in her hurry to get past her pain, could she have confused things and made assumptions?

For a moment, she might allow herself to imagine Oliver *did* find her desirable.

He had kissed her that one time, after all.

Over the last two years, she had caught Oliver staring at her. And it hadn't been with disgust. It had been with…could it have been with hunger?

He trembled sometimes when she touched his hand or hugged him.

He did not seek the company of other women. He had sold the remainder of his father's businesses over a year ago and no longer went to London. And she did not think he could hide a mistress in so small a place as Woldenmere.

And this afternoon…had that really been a handkerchief in his other hand? It had been far too large. And there had been a bit of blue mixed in with the white.

She had a chemise with a blue ribbon for the drawstring in the neckline.

She lit a lamp and got up and went to her clothes press to look for that particular chemise. She couldn't find it. She remembered wearing it last week, putting it in the pile of things to be washed, but she didn't remember ever hanging it up with the other laundry to dry.

It had disappeared.

She tapped her fingertips against her mouth, trying to contain her hope. *Don't let your mind run wild with silly impossibilities, Hen.*

But it was too late. She could not rein back the notion that maybe she had gotten everything all wrong. Maybe he had said he would not fornicate with her because he had thought her unwilling. He had thought he had forced that kiss on her. Or maybe he had thought her too young. All of which was nonsense, of course.

I will not impose on you.

If only she had been brave enough to say by the ha-ha, "It would be no imposition, at all. I fancy you. I fancy everything about you."

But she had been much too intimidated by him back then.

It had taken all her courage to contradict him and to assert she absolutely was going to care for Nathaniel.

And despite feeling much more comfortable with Oliver now, she still didn't think she could come right out and tell him she desired him.

But this was ridiculous! Two adult people, married to each other, not expressing physical love. She should march into his room right now and demand her marital rights!

No, she couldn't do that. If she were wrong and he didn't want her…oh, she'd die of shame and embarrassment. The friendly, cozy fellowship they had between them—the thing that made her happiest—might vanish.

Henrietta went back to her bed but couldn't find sleep. She'd always tried hard to be content with herself and not to spend too much time longing to be different, but how she wished right now she had been born clever so she could puzzle this out.

She must find a way to sound Oliver out on the subject of copulating with her. But in a safely roundabout manner that couldn't possibly reveal her true feelings for him.

Could she pretend to sleepwalk into his room one night and get into bed with him? No, after two years of having adjoining bedchambers, he knew she didn't sleepwalk.

She could ask him to take her somewhere. Cornwall. York. Anywhere. And there might be a crowded coaching inn. And only one room and only one bed. They would have to share, and she would feign sleep and drape herself over him and see what came to pass.

No. Knowing her resourceful and efficient husband, he would find another room, another bed, no matter how full the inn.

If only Oliver were a duke like her father and needed an heir for his title. But even then, Oliver had Nathaniel already. No need for an heir. No need for Henrietta to reproduce.

No. Yes.

Yes, that was it. Because she *would* like to have babies. It wasn't a pressing need—not nearly as pressing as her lust for Oliver—but she did want more children in their family someday. Maybe someday was now?

She'd ask him for a child. Not a bedding, but a baby. She'd see what he said.

Having a plan settled her, and she finally slept.

She waited a week. She didn't want Oliver to make the embarrassing connection between her seeing his phallus and her asking for a baby.

She broached the subject after dinner, in the drawing room, while he read his newspaper and she embroidered.

"I want a child."

He didn't say anything for a long time. If it had been anyone else, she would have been worried he was laughing at her behind the newspaper. But not Oliver. She knew he was thinking, considering, weighing.

Finally, he put the newspaper aside and looked at her intently.

First, she was too young. Next, he was too old.

Then, he surprised her by discussing pleasure. She tried to be as honest with him as she could be. But it was all mixed together in her mind. His release. The one she had given herself afterwards. Holding a little baby with dark hair. The dreams she'd had about him for so long.

He promised her he would think on it. She knew he'd come to a decision that was right for him, for her, for Nathaniel. Oh, was it selfish to hope the right decision was the one she wanted?

Probably.

She didn't have to wait long. When she came back from

her morning ride the very next day, he was standing outside the stables. He looked exhausted, as if he hadn't slept.

"Good morning," she called out.

"Good morning," he replied. "I was hoping to speak with you before we break our fast."

After she had dismounted and left Zephyr in the hands of a groom, she joined him.

"Let's take a stroll," he said. "If that's all right?"

She nodded, and they walked silently next to each other, down the lane.

"I've never seen you ride," he said.

He hadn't?

"You have a very good seat. But I didn't expect…you ride at quite a fast pace. I didn't know a draft horse could fly like that."

"Yes. We love to gallop, and Zephyr is like the wind. That's how he got his name."

A pause. "Were you using the saddle you made?"

"Oh, no, that's…no."

Silence.

"You look tired, Oliver."

"I have been considering your proposal."

She had caused those dark circles under his eyes, the deepening of the grooves by the side of his mouth. Oh, how she longed to touch his face with her fingertips and soothe away those lines and shadows.

He went on, his voice somber. "Nathaniel's mother, she died because— Bearing a child is a dangerous undertaking."

"Yes, but lots of women have children and survive. My mother, five times. And aren't most things worth doing also a little dangerous?"

He grimaced. "Like riding your horse so fast?"

Oh, yes. Oliver hated danger. Last month, Nathaniel had gotten it into his head to climb a tree like the caterpillar in her story. She thought he could try the sturdy oak with thick limbs not a yard off the ground, and she was there, ready to give him a boost if needed, ready to catch him. But Oliver had seen and raced from the house and pulled Nathaniel off the tree, scaring the boy.

He hadn't scolded Henrietta right away, even though she could see he was furious. He had waited until Nathaniel was in the nursery with Nurse Witherspoon, and then the two of them had had a long conversation in his study about what Nathaniel could or couldn't do. It was the closest thing to an argument they'd ever had.

After Henrietta had explained how young all her brothers and sisters had been when they had started climbing trees, Oliver had relented but said he wanted to have a good talk first with Nathaniel about never climbing anything unless Oliver was there.

"Or me," Henrietta had said.

He had studied her for several long seconds as if assessing her strength, her agility, her *love* for Nathaniel, and then said, "Or you."

But this was not the time to have a conversation about how safe it was for her to ride her horse.

She skirted a rut in the lane and looked across the meadow towards Woldenmere.

"I'm sorry. So sorry for upsetting everything. We can forget I ever said anything."

"No. I don't want to forget what you said."

He spoke as he usually did, with very little emotion, but she knew better than to think he had no feelings on the subject.

"Would you mind terribly being a father again?"

He did not answer for a long time. He looked at the sky.

"Not if you're the mother."

She couldn't help smiling. And despite wanting him to

believe she was very much a grown woman and not a girl, she skipped a little, right there in the lane, right next to him.

She didn't care he might only have been offering a tribute to her as a stepmother. She didn't even care she still had no idea if he desired her.

She was so happy.

She had given him a way to escape, to retreat, and he hadn't taken it. Oliver Hartwell, at long last, was going to bed his wife.

Fifteen

A knock woke her from sleep.

"Come in," she mumbled.

The door connecting her bedchamber to Oliver's bedchamber opened. A lamp was lit in his room, and as she squinted into the light, she could see his tall, lean form standing in the doorway.

"Oliver?"

"I'm sorry to have disturbed your sleep. Good night, Henrietta." The door started to close.

"No!"

If she had not been naked under the sheets, she would have leapt from the bed to drag him into the room.

She had departed the drawing room what must have been hours ago, giving him a hopeful look as she left. Lucy had put her in a nightdress and taken her hair down and plaited it, and once her lady's maid had bid her goodnight, Henrietta had quickly stripped the nightdress off, shaken loose the plait, given herself a quick wash at the basin, turned the lamp down, and scrambled into bed to wait for Oliver in the dark.

Because when she had asked him for a child yesterday evening, she had also promised him the dark, hadn't she? Even though she was dying to look at him. So she mustn't put him off now with her flesh. She mustn't remind him she wasn't small and delicate like his previous wives. That might spoil everything.

"Please, Oliver." She tried to keep desperation out of her voice. "I'm not asleep. Well, I drifted off a bit, waiting for you, but I'm awake now. See?"

The door stayed half-closed. "Yes."

"Please, let's get this over with. I'm awfully anxious."

An odd, strangled noise came from the doorway. Had he laughed?

"Only you could be awfully anxious and still fall asleep."

Oh. Oh. How delightful. She rubbed her toes together under the bedclothes in a little dance of joy. Her serious husband had teased her.

"You know me." She'd meant to say it in a friendly way, but it came out as an almost-seductive purr.

He cleared his throat. "Forgive me. I'm very nervous myself."

Oliver was nervous? Even though he had done this before?

"Don't be nervous. It's just me, after all."

Another strange noise came from him. Oh, no. Was he going to flee?

"Please, come in. Won't you? Please?"

At first, his silhouette did not move. Then there was a step, and the light behind him winked out as the door closed, and they were in the dark together.

She got up on her elbows. "You'll have to tell me if I do something wrong. I'm not the most clever, as you know, and I don't want to…I mean, I want you to enjoy it."

"You're very clever. And I should be the one trying to make sure you enjoy it."

How sweet he was being. She swallowed. "I'm sure I'll like anything you do."

"I am…*not* sure you will."

"I liked your kiss," she said boldly.

He said nothing.

"The kiss you gave me? In my father's study?"

"I remember."

She waited as long as she could. Many seconds. "So, are you going to come into the bed?"

"Yes."

Rustling followed, and she cursed the darkness, longing to light a candle. She wanted to watch her husband undress, see those long limbs in all their glory. See his skin. See his member again and find out if he was aroused as he had been when she had seen it before.

The mattress dipped as he slipped in under the sheet and counterpane, carefully keeping to the other side of the bed, not touching her, not even accidentally.

She smelled something familiar.

"I've always wondered," she said.

"What?"

"That kiss…your mouth tasted of…well, I've never had whisky, but I've smelled it on my father's breath before. Had you drunk some whisky that night you kissed me?"

"Yes."

"Did you drink some tonight?"

"One glass. I thought it might help my nerves."

"Has it?"

"I think I might still be downstairs if not for the whisky."

She turned on her side, towards him, wanting to touch him so badly. "Perhaps you should have drunk more than one glass."

"Whisky can impede…performance."

"Is that true for women?"

"There's no question of performance for women, is there?"

She lifted her shoulders, even though he could not possibly see her shrug in the dark. "I don't know. I don't even really understand what you mean by performance. Isn't it something we're meant to do together?"

He coughed. "You are experienced."

It wasn't a question.

"What?" she choked out.

"Last night, when you asked for a child, you said women can have pleasure during the act. And I thought—"

"You thought I had…?"

"Haven't you?"

She fought against her tears with a rare burst of temper. "I have had one experience with a man. One. My husband kissed me in my father's study. Of course, he wasn't my husband then. I suppose that makes me a wanton."

Then she did cry. Oh, no. She had been on the brink of having physical intimacy with Oliver, and she had ruined it.

Or maybe not.

He gathered her to him. At first, she didn't notice he was wearing a shirt as he put those heavenly forearms around her, pressed her into his chest, and said, "Forgive me. I'm a fool."

But after several sobs, she didn't like the scratch of the linen against her face, the fact her bare breasts were not against his skin. His clothing was as offensive to her as his presumption she was not a virgin.

"You're wearing a shirt," she said through her tears.

"I…I didn't know what you would want."

"I'm naked."

He didn't speak for a while. "I know. That. Now." His voice was as strangled and raspy as it had been after he had spent by his own hand.

She snuffled. "Can you be naked, too?"

"As you wish."

He released her and there was a whiffle through the air and when he put his arms around her again, her cheek settled against hot skin covered with hair. Hair on his chest. Mmmmm.

"That's so much better, Oliver."

He said nothing, so she nuzzled her face into his chest and dared to kiss him there. Under her lips, she could feel his heart beating almost as rapidly as hers was.

"There's something you should know," he said.

Mmmmm. His skin tasted as good as it smelled. She kissed his chest again.

"I…neither of my…I am not…don't worry, I should be able to impregnate you, it should be no problem whatsoever, but I am almost certain you will not enjoy it."

She stopped kissing his chest. "I'm enjoying this. You holding me. Kissing your skin."

"About that…"

"Yes?"

"I think I had better perform my duty now."

That must be his way of saying he didn't enjoy the holding and the kissing. She'd have to learn what he liked in this, just as she had with other parts of their life together.

She rolled onto her back.

"All right," she said. "I'm ready."

The devil take him, he should have drunk the whole damn bottle of whisky. He was brimming, on the verge of coming, and he hadn't even let his cock touch her, angling his lower half away from her as he held her gorgeous body.

If he didn't use every ounce of restraint he possessed, he would spill outside of her and she wouldn't get the baby she wanted. But Henrietta was accommodating, willing to go along with his undue haste.

He felt he should warn her. "There can be pain."

"Yes, I know. My mother told me a great deal about it all. Everything."

Her mother. Of course, Georgiana would educate her daughters. Oliver should never have supposed Henrietta had already experienced copulation. Yet another regret in a long line of his regrettable actions towards her.

And the duchess was probably the one to mislead Henrietta about pleasure during the act. Oliver knew from hints Crispin had dropped over the last two decades that he and Georgiana had the vanishingly rare experience of sharing a fervent and mutual desire in their marriage bed.

"But the pain has to do with breaking something, doesn't it?" Henrietta asked. "I ride so much, surely I'm already broken?"

He had not thought of that. Maybe this would be less uncomfortable for her than it had been for Violet who had screamed curses at him the first time or Emily who had cried silently.

He moved towards her under the sheet and got on his knees.

He could actually hear her swallow before she whispered, "What should I do?"

"Can you spread your legs?"

Obediently, she slid her legs apart, and he moved his knees into the gap she had created on the mattress. He leaned down and put a hand flat on either side of her. The wet tip of his cock brushed against the soft skin of her belly, and he hissed.

"Sorry," he said just as she said, "Are you all right?"and lifted her head and knocked her forehead against his.

If only he were the type who could laugh at their mutual clumsiness and assure her everything was fine.

But he wasn't. And damn it, he did not think he could afford to delay any longer. Still hovering over her, he took one hand and held his cock and tried to find her entrance.

"Oh," she said and sucked in a breath. "That's lovely." She wriggled just a little. "You touching me there."

It was more than lovely. It was tremendous, tantalizing, titillating to brush his fingers and the head of his cock over her heated lips and their soft wisps of hair. And deeper in, she was wet in her delicate folds and not just from his own persistent dribble.

"May I?" he said through clenched teeth.

"Yes. Please."

He put the head of his cock just barely inside her. God, he was close.

"Is that all right?" he gasped out.

Her hands came up and rested on his shoulders. "Anything you do is all right, Oliver."

That wasn't true. That had never been true. Nevertheless, he slowly pressed into her. Her sex was ungodly hot and tight, gripping him.

She made a little sound.

"Am I hurting you?"

"Yes, I mean, it's a full feeling. But, please, don't stop." Her hands moved from his shoulders to his upper arms. "Please."

He slid in farther, clenching his buttocks in the hopes that would keep him from release.

"Yes," she said.

Another inch from him. *Oh, my God*. And then another, and another, and another and suddenly he was totally seated in her, totally surrounded by her.

"Is that it?" she said, her voice a little strained. "Is it over?"

Almost, he wanted to say. Instead, he ground out, "I'm going to pull back and push in again."

Her hands tightened on his arms. "You have to start again? I did something wrong."

Her mother's lessons must not have been as comprehensive as Henrietta had said.

"You did nothing wrong. No. It's part of the…it's normal."

"I see."

He eased himself backwards, her sultry tightness pulling at him, squeezing him. At the very end of his stroke, he felt the tingle in his spine and quickly thrust into her again, sheathing himself completely and…*Oh, my God. Oh, my God. Oh. My. God.* He exploded into her. Rapture. Bliss. He saw stars in the dark room.

When he regained any semblance of reason, he was still lodged in her, suspended over her, panting, covered in a sheen of sweat, her hands on his upper arms.

He drew in a deep breath. "It's over now." He felt some of his seed spilling out as he withdrew his member. Her hands fell away, and he moved to her side on his knees.

"Are you all right?" he asked, cringing in the dark, preparing himself for her anger, her tears, her disappointment.

"Yes. Thank you, Oliver. Thank you."

She was thanking him, he supposed, for the child she might conceive. It couldn't be because she had enjoyed any part of that. Best he depart now.

"I'll let you sleep." He moved to get out of the bed.

"No," she yelped and in the dark, a strong grip latched onto his forearm. "I mean…aren't you going to sleep here? Please?"

He'd never slept in the same bed as someone else, except as a child when he had gone to his nurse's bed with a nightmare. Violet hadn't wanted anything to do with him before, during, or after coition, and Emily had never invited him to sleep with her. Even if she had, Emily was so frail, he would have feared injuring her.

"I might roll over in my sleep and hurt you."

Henrietta laughed. "You couldn't hurt me."

That was true. She was beautifully strong and solid. Lovely, well, and alive.

Suddenly, desperately, he wanted to do something for her. He wanted to care for the woman who cared for everyone around her.

"Let me get a cloth for you to clean yourself."

"All right."

He could see the outlines of the table where her basin and pitcher sat. He felt around the table and came up with two cloths. He dampened them and cleaned himself with one and brought the other one back to the bed.

"Here."

She fumbled and found the wet cloth in his hand and took it. "Wiping away the seed won't interfere?"

Again, her mother's lessons hadn't taught her everything. "No. There's plenty deep inside you."

There was some movement and rustling and she handed the cloth back to him.

"You will come back to bed with me, won't you?"

"Yes." He took the cloth to the basin and went back to the bed and slid in next to her. Suddenly, he felt her hand holding his.

"Thank you, Oliver."

He lay awake for several hours while she slept. He got hard again with the thought of her naked body next to his, just inches away. But eventually he drifted off, her hand still in his.

He came out of sleep just before dawn to a bouquet of red curls in his face and a lush, warm armful of woman against him, her breasts hugging his side, one of her perfect, dimpled thighs sprawled over both of his. Carefully, he extracted himself, gathered his shirt and the rest of his clothes, and fled to his own room before she could wake.

In the light of day, she might not be able to hide her displeasure from him, what she really felt about what he had done to her in the dark.

He needed to dress, to shave, to erect his usual shields before he would have the courage to face her.

Sixteen

Henrietta woke up alone. But Oliver had been there for most of the night, she was sure of it.

So. That was fornication.

In so many ways, it had been just like a stallion mounting a mare. Just as brief, just as passionless.

It certainly hadn't been what she had imagined it would be based on her mother's descriptions. Or based on her own thoughts when she touched herself.

She'd liked the first part. Whispering in the dark. Smelling the whisky on his breath. Him holding her. Her kissing his chest.

The next part? Well, she thought she might like to have that full feeling again, and she'd liked his body being close to hers, but there'd been scarcely any touching. And it was so quick. And he really hadn't gotten that close to her pleasure spot, had he?

She'd thought of giving herself some relief afterwards, but she didn't know if it would disturb either him or his seed if she touched herself down there, so she had refrained. And she had promised him she would like anything he did, so it didn't seem like a good idea to touch herself and demonstrate to him that he had not satisfied her.

Even though he hadn't. Nowhere near.

Still, she had had the pleasure of the holding before and the sleeping next to him after. And she might get a child from this.

It was a pity the ecstasy he gave her heart was not matched by an ecstasy he gave her body.

Yet.

She touched herself between her legs. Yes, her entrance was sore. She shifted over to look at the sheet under where her bottom had been. Yes, no blood. It had been just as she had guessed—she had had nothing to break and therefore there had been no reason for her to bleed.

Now she was lying where Oliver's body had been, where he had slept. She turned over and buried her face in the pillow where his head had rested. Oh, the delicious scent of him.

And there face down, she wormed a hand under her belly and rubbed herself, breathing deeply through her nose and thinking about him.

Surrounded by his smell, she had one of the most glorious climaxes of her life.

Oh, Oliver.

If only he had held her longer. Kissed her. Touched her breasts. Touched her between her legs more.

But he was so much older, so much wiser, so much more experienced. There couldn't possibly be anything she could teach him. He had done this with at least two other women. He must know what he was doing, right?

Right?

That evening, after dinner, she developed a new worry.

"I don't suppose," she said, staring into the fire. It was

rainy. They were in the drawing room. He was reading his newspaper, but she had not yet taken up her stitchery.

"Mmm?" he said from behind his paper.

"Well," she said and straightened her skirts. "I don't suppose—that is, after I am with child, you might continue to come to my bed?"

He moved his paper to the side. His gray eyes flared with a strange heat as he quirked one eyebrow at her. And there was that one lock of hair suspended over his forehead. That gorgeous curl. She'd love to touch it. It looked so soft and thick.

"I would not wish to inconvenience you," he said.

Inconvenience was just another word for *impose*. But this time, she wouldn't stay silent. She would make it clear he should come to her.

"You wouldn't inconvenience me. I mean, there's a bit of a mess, isn't there? But that's easily cleaned up. And it would be warm and cozy in the winter. So very pleasant."

Even if there would be no ecstasy for her in her marital duty, there would be physical closeness and, she hoped, some pleasure for her husband. And although he had not been effusive about that pleasure—when was he ever effusive about anything?—she had liked giving it to him.

She wanted to be the one to give it to him.

He cleared his throat. "I see. Yes, it would be warm."

"But not *too* warm. Just right. Even in the summer," she said, thinking ahead for once. She didn't want him not to come to her in the hotter months.

Now it was his turn to stare into the fire. "I take it you did not enjoy the act."

"Yes, yes, I did." She felt herself blush. "What made you say that?"

"Your choice of words. *Warm* and *cozy* and *pleasant*."

"Those are good words," she said indignantly.

"Yes, they are." He went back to reading his paper.

"You didn't answer my question."

"I'm thinking."

She dearly wished she could see his face behind the newspaper. "What are you thinking about?"

"I'd rather not say."

"Oh."

He folded his paper down. "It's too soon to know if you are with child. So, the question doesn't need an answer yet."

"Yes, it's far too soon." But when would she know? She counted on her fingers. At least she had the assurance he would come to her bed—oh, at least ten more times. Her courses were very regular and as soon as she missed a day— well, their time in bed together might end.

Until she wanted another child.

He watched her touch her own fingers in some mysterious dance and wondered what they'd feel like on his cock.

Jesus.

He flipped his paper back up before he became any more aroused just looking at her.

Warm and *pleasant* and *cozy*. Pleasant, for God's sake! When he had been as hard as granite and brimming over as soon as he got into the bed, panicked he would spill just touching her.

Oliver turned the page of his newspaper, frowning.

Yesterday, he would have been happy she had said it was *pleasant*. Anything would have been better than *vile*, which is what Violet had said it was.

No, Henrietta hadn't been revolted like Violet had been. She hadn't been scared and mute like Emily. He had been a fool to think Henrietta would be. She was not Violet nor Emily.

However, he was still himself. A failure, now and forever. He had provoked nothing in her except *cozy* and *pleasant*. And *warm*.

Damn, he was worthless. He was a hot water bottle, not a husband.

"I wish," she said.

"You wish what?" he bit out, still stewing in his anger at himself.

"I wish you'd tell me what you're thinking." Her voice was as calm and soft as it was when she told a story to his son. "I never know what you're thinking. But I'm your wife. A real wife now, because we know each other, like in the Bible. I should know your thoughts, too, shouldn't I?"

His innocent wife—yes, still innocent, despite the fact he had spent inside her last night—wanted to know his thoughts?

"Please, Oliver. Please tell me what you're thinking. I want to know."

She wanted to know.

And he had vowed to give her anything she wanted.

He threw the paper down, and he threw caution to the winds. He leaned forward, almost coming out of the chair, and spilled out the filth that befouled his mind.

"I'm thinking I want to rip every shred of clothing off you and ravish you right here. I'm thinking I want to suckle at your big, gorgeous breasts until you leak milk into my mouth. I'm thinking I want to wrap your thighs around my neck while I kneel at your feet and feast on your cunt and lick you and tongue you and bury my face in your sweetness as you pull my hair and scream my name. I'm thinking I want to plunge my hard prick into you over and over and over again like a savage animal until you're delirious with ecstasy and your pussy squeezes around me and you come on my cock while I explode inside your womb."

She trembled. No, she quaked. Large, jerky movements

from her head all the way down to her slippered feet that beat out a stuttering tattoo on the carpet. Every bit of her exposed skin turned red, an even deeper shade than her hair. Her eyes widened and her pupils became enormous, turning her pale-blue irises into mere rims surrounding inky pools.

"Well," she gasped.

He gasped, too. He could not believe what he had just said to her. To the purest piece of sweetness and goodness in existence.

Violet had been right. He *was* vile. The things that had just come out of his mouth would embarrass a stevedore, let alone a barely deflowered maiden.

He threw himself back into the chair, wiping the spittle from his mouth. His own words had engorged his cock to the point of pain. And he deserved that pain.

She would flee now. Because she had asked what he was thinking and he had told her.

Maybe she would just flee figuratively, withdrawing her request for a child, for copulation, for his company in any guise.

Maybe she would flee literally, back to her parents, abandoning Nathaniel when she was the only mother he had ever known. And she would abandon Oliver, too.

A terrible error in judgment two years ago had brought him so much happiness. He had fallen into something good, for once. And now another error in judgment had destroyed it.

His old companions darkness and despondency were just beginning to settle over him when he heard her say something under her breath.

"Why don't you?"

His eyes snapped to hers. "What did you say?"

"I said." She blinked several times and then spoke loudly

and clearly, enunciating every word carefully. "Why don't you do what you're thinking?"

"You don't know what you're asking," he snarled, completely powerless to pretend at niceties any longer.

"I know," she said, her voice now tremulous. "I know… your words, what you just said to me, the pictures you put in my head…I liked it."

He swallowed.

"I more than liked it." She licked her lips. "I ache for you. For your," she hesitated, "cock."

With the agility of youth, she was suddenly out of her chair and kneeling at his feet and undoing his fall that strained to hold his throbbing member in abeyance.

"What—"

She tore at his buttons until his groin was bared, his hard shaft springing out, fully erect.

Unerringly, her fingers wrapped around him. The first erotic touch ever on his cock from a hand that wasn't his own.

"I'm going to do what *I'm* thinking." Now she was the one with spittle flying from her mouth, a feral gleam in her eye as she looked up at him and moved her hand over his shaft. "I'm thinking about how I saw you," she moved her hand faster, "do this and I realized I had to have you. Have your prick."

"You…you don't want a baby?"

"I'm greedy. I want you, I want your cock, I want your babies, I want—" She stopped herself from speaking. Stopped her movement of her hand along his length. Bit her lip. "I want everything."

"I—"

"I want you to spend on my face."

He looked down at her beautiful face. The face of a goddess. Not a chaste Artemis or Athena. But a wild, wanton temptress of the highest order. Aphrodite. She'd always been that, hadn't she? A true voluptuary. The way she savored her food, thrilled to a vigorous ride through the countryside, relished a cool breeze on her skin.

He had persisted in boxing her in. Persisted in thinking her a child. Why? When he had allowed her to be the woman who was a mother to his son, the woman who ran his household.

He had been making her smaller than she really was. When really she was…utterly magnificent.

Her hand began to move again and there was no room for thought anymore, only the most urgent need. He was rising to a peak that towered over every fell.

She had been looking up at his face but then her rosy-gold lashes fluttered, her blue eyes disappeared as her neck bent, and she said, "You said you wanted to feast on me. Well, I want to feast on you."

She took him in her mouth.

Oh, my God. Her mouth. Hot and wet like her quim had been last night despite his incompetence as a lover. His hips bucked, lurched, and thrust as she sucked at him and swirled her tongue over his tip like it was a spoonful of her favorite ice and her hand continued to move up and down as if she were feeding herself his shaft.

"Henrietta. I'm going to—" was all he got out as a warning and then it was upon him.

His first spurt landed far back in her throat, but she released him from her mouth and pulled her head back and the rest landed where she wanted it.

On her round cheeks. Her freckled nose.

Her perfect face was covered in his seed. Seed spent for pleasure only, not for a baby.

"Oh, my God," he said out loud.

Her hand came away from his cock. Moments ago, during the act of pleasuring him, she had been bold and brazen. But now worry returned to her, and her forehead furrowed.

"Was that all right?"

His mind was blank. But it mustn't be. He must say something to her. Summon words. Praise.

"That," he dared to lay his hands on the face of his daring wife, "was more than all right. That was unbelievable." He ran a thumb through his spend on her cheek, and the anxiousness faded from her eyes. "Unbelievable pleasure. You just gave me. I thank you."

"I must be a mess." But now her voice wasn't fretful. It was husky, without a trace of regret. Almost taunting.

"A beautiful mess," he corrected her as he took out his handkerchief and cleaned her face gently.

She just stared up at him.

He took her hands and stood, drawing her up with him, his braces holding up his trousers as his fall flapped open.

Looming over her, he walked her backwards. She fell into her own chair with a little puff of surprise. He knelt at her feet and drew her skirts and petticoats up to her waist. Her round knees were together. He gently pushed them apart from each other, separating those plump thighs that belied the underlying muscle that kept her on her horse.

And then she was open to him, and he saw her beautiful sex that he had only felt in the dark last night. Tight, copper curls framing her dark-pink pudenda, glistening in the firelight.

She was wet for him.

Her fingers found his shoulders. He looked up from her gorgeous sex and said, "I've never—"

"I haven't either, as you know," she said quickly. "None of this."

"So you'll have to help me. Tell me if you don't like anything—"

"You, too."

"But I've dreamed of this with you. I've wanted this with you."

Still keeping his eyes on hers, he leaned in and kissed the inside of one stockinged knee. Slowly, he kissed his way up her thigh. When he got close to the top of the stocking, he had to force his eyes away from her face due to the angle of his neck. When he got past the garter and kissed her bare skin for the first time, he heard her whimper.

It cut straight to his heart, dissecting away the scars of being despised, of being unwanted by two other women.

He had planned to kiss his way down her other thigh, but once he got close to her quim, he couldn't move away. Her sweet musk was intoxicating. Part Pears soap, part sweat, part saddle leather, but mostly something that must be her arousal. Essence of Henrietta. He brought both of his hands up and gently parted her outer lips. He kissed the pink, dewed flesh around her entrance. More whimpers. He nudged with his nose as he kissed and finally brought out his tongue and gave her a long lick, all the way to the top of her sex.

"Ooooooooh. There. There. That's it. That's it." Her hands laced into his hair.

"You like that?" he said into her cunt, reveling in her heady taste and dizzy with the notion that she actually wanted him to do this.

"The top, that little place at the top, that's the place where…if you touch me there, I'll spend. I mean that's what I do on my own…"

Henrietta gave herself pleasure. Of course she did. His sensual voluptuary would not deny herself just because she had married a coward.

He felt with his tongue around the top of her slit and there was a little nub of hardness there.

She yelped. "That's it, that's it."

Vasco da Gama had nothing on him. Nor Ponce de

León, nor Captain Cook. Who gave a fuck about the Fountain of Life? The source of the Nile? The Northwest Passage?

Oliver Hartwell had discovered the source of his wife's greatest pleasure.

"Gentle at first," she whispered.

With the lightest touch, he licked the nub. Her fingers momentarily released his hair and then pulled.

"Yes, Oliver. Oliver!"

He licked a bit harder. She squealed. He licked faster. For the first time ever, he heard his wife take the Lord's name in vain. The little nub was getting harder and harder and larger. He dipped down to her entrance. Her juices were copious now and he needed a taste of her there. And as he tongued her entrance, he felt his phallus begin to revive. His forty-three year old cock was ready for more, was it?

She quieted. But as he returned to the nub and set up the pulsing quick rhythm of his tongue again, she squealed. Again.

"God, God, God. Oliver. Oliver. Oliver!"

Her legs shook, her fingers mauled his head, she commingled his name with the almighty's. Then she collapsed, quivering. He kissed her outer lips lightly, not ready to leave this brave, new world.

Finally, he straightened and sat back on his haunches. His height meant he had had to bend down quite a bit to get to her quim. His fantasy hadn't taken that into account. He must buy some chairs with taller legs.

Her eyes were on him, but they were dreamy, hazed, far away in some land of indolent pleasure.

"Goodness," she breathed.

Creakily, he got to his feet and buttoned his fall over his once-again tumescent organ. She bit her lip as she watched him put himself away.

"But…but what about the suckling of my breasts and the plunging into me like you're a wild beast?"

He leaned over and pulled down her skirts. "Let's go upstairs and take care of that in a bed. You make my cock think it's twenty years old, but the rest of me isn't."

A hearty laugh burst from her before she pressed her lips together in a futile attempt to control her merriment. "Will you say more lewd things to me?"

He leaned over again and put his hands on the arms of the chair and got his face very close to hers. "Do you want me tell you about how I want you on your hands and knees on the mattress so I can take you from behind while I grope your sinfully gorgeous bottom? Drive my cock into you from that position so forcefully that your beautiful flesh jiggles and shakes and you collapse onto the bed, crushed by my need for you?"

She stared at him, her mouth agape. "Yes."

He straightened his back and groaned and held out his hand. "Then come with me, wife."

SEVENTEEN

Hand in hand, he took her to her bedchamber, the same room they had coupled in last night, but now everything was different.

He wanted all the lamps lit.

"I want to see you. You're so beautiful."

She felt her face get hot.

"When I say you're beautiful, Henrietta, I mean it. All of you. Even the parts I haven't seen yet."

She ducked her head. "If you haven't seen those parts, how do you know they're beautiful?"

He put a hand under her chin and gently lifted so she had to look at him. "I know."

She hoped it was true. She had believed for so long he did not find her desirable.

"Will you let me undress you?" he asked.

She hated to deny him, but she shook her head. Something wasn't right. They had been husband and wife for two years. Eaten almost all of their meals together. Shared the raising of a child. And now they had engaged in some very intimate activities together.

But he hadn't kissed her except the one time. In her father's study. When she had been too startled to appreciate it.

It might have taken her a long while, but she had finally learned she must ask her husband for what she *really* wanted.

She dropped her gaze to his mouth, surrounded by the dark scruff of his evening whiskers. His narrow, sculpted lips were so unlike her own wide, plump ones.

"Will you kiss me?" she asked those lips.

For the first time in her life, she saw his lips broaden and curve up into a smile. Then they said, "I very much want to."

He came closer to her. One of his large hands went to the nape of her neck, cradling her head. His other arm wrapped around her waist and his hand settled on the middle of her back.

He pulled her against his hard, lean torso, and she felt herself dissolving, her form molding to his, as if their two vastly different bodies were meant to fit together. Perhaps they were.

Suddenly nervous of making a misstep, she slowly brought her arms up and around his neck. She had to tilt her head back so she could continue to look at his mouth. He slanted his own head slightly as his face descended. For a second, he teased her, his smiling lips hovering over hers and she smelled his heated breath.

No whisky. Just the scent of Oliver and her own desire.

Then his lips pressed against hers as his hand on her back pressed her into him even more securely.

At first, his lips were relaxed and gentle. But as time went on, they became fierce and possessive, roaming over her mouth, claiming her lips, owning them. She felt the warm wetness of his tongue stroke against her mouth and she opened to it, welcoming it in. She wanted him, all of him, she wanted anything he gave her. And his tongue was wickedly provocative, probing into her, tasting her, giving her a taste of herself, reminding her of what that tongue had just done between her own legs.

His grip on her nape tightened. She dared to lick his lips, explore his mouth a little, and he groaned into her kiss and she could feel his length hardening against her.

Their mouths were joined for a long time. But she wanted the kiss to last forever. When he broke away and fingered a curl that had tumbled down next to her face, some embarrassingly greedy sound escaped from her before she could swallow it back and her arms tightened around his neck and she went up on her toes. Her husband smiled—another smile!—at her flagrant desire and kissed her once again.

This time, he took her mouth with a driving force. She felt herself bending back with the passion of this kiss. He was consuming her, ravishing her, and her limbs, her belly, all of her had turned into liquid fire.

His lips went to her neck, searing her skin next to her jaw, and she whispered, "You can undress me now."

"I'm sorely tempted to take you like this and undress you afterwards." He pulled her upright and spun her around to begin unbuttoning her dress. "But I'm not going to do that. I am going to take my time. I am going to see all of you. I am going to worship all of you. And I'm going to tell you every lascivious thought that comes into my head."

"I want to hear your thoughts," she said and whimpered when he kissed the back of her neck. "All of them."

"Even the filthy ones that involve debauching my wife?" he whispered into her ear.

"Especially those."

His long, strong fingers soon had her dress unbuttoned and off, her stays unlaced and removed, and she stood in her chemise, petticoat, stockings, slippers.

"Will you turn around for me?" he asked from behind her, his hands on her hips.

She turned and was startled by him bearing down on her again as his arms wrapped around her and he gave her a brutal, ravening kiss.

"I've waited too long to kiss you, and now I can't stop."

"I hope you never stop," she said between kisses as his hands came up and held the sides of her breasts, now unrestrained and only covered by her thin chemise.

The liquid fire began to concentrate itself between her legs and in her nipples as the holding turned into gentle squeezing, his large hands taking possession of her equally large breasts.

"So beautiful. These are so beautiful. You are so beautiful."

He bent his neck and still holding her breasts, he trailed his lips over the top of her bosom. His head sank lower and found a nipple and began to suck at it through her chemise.

His hot mouth, the light nip of his teeth, the pull of his lips brought a sensation to her breast that had the piercing quality of pain, quickly overwhelmed by a heated wash of pleasure. Her head went back, and she clutched at him.

"I can't…"

He released her breast from his mouth, a look of panic on his face. "What? What can't you do?"

"I can't stand."

She wasn't sure how it happened, but somehow he got her next to the bed, and she fell onto the mattress.

"Perfection. Pure perfection," he muttered, looking down at her. Then he was leaning over her, removing her petticoat, slippers, and stockings.

His hands went to his cravat. "The shift is coming off, too."

She nodded, mutely. She had no objections, but she was not going to risk missing a moment of his undressing. The lamps were lit for her, too. She wanted to see her husband. She wanted to watch.

Swiftly, efficiently, everything came off his body and the man of her dreams stood in front of her.

Long and lean. Almost bronzed on his face and neck and forearms where his skin was often in the sun and a pale gold everywhere else. Dark hair on his chest and forearms and legs. And yes, that same dark hair at the base of his jutting, hard cock. But that was the part of his body she had seen the most. She wanted to see and feel everything else, too. She knelt on the edge of the bed.

"Please, will you come to me?"

He stepped forward and stood in front of her as she ran her hands over him and explored her husband's body.

In so many ways, he had the form of a much younger man. Taut skin and lean muscle and sharp bone.

She started at his shoulders. Perfectly square, and even if they were narrow, they were the widest part of his slim body. And just underneath, his collarbone was a graceful line. She ran her hands down his upper arms. The skin was so smooth. She reached the forearms she adored. She lifted each one and pressed a kiss to the rapid pulse in his wrists.

Now back to his chest. Hard under the curling, wiry, dark hair. The flat abdomen, the narrow waist and hips. Her thumbs caressed his protruding hip bones.

"I love these," she said. "I don't have these."

He laughed and she looked up and his face was red. Oliver was blushing? Oliver was laughing?

"You do have them," he said.

"Well, I can't feel mine. They're padded."

"Padded exquisitely with your beautiful flesh." Then, finally revealing a bit of impatience. "Are you finished?"

"No."

His cock jerked, begging for her attention, so she gave it a kiss on the tip. He hissed.

"But you like that, right?" she asked, looking up.

His face was stoic. "Yes."

The soft sac below. She touched it, held it in her hand like he had held her breasts. He groaned.

"Is this sensitive as well?"

"Yes, but not as much."

And now she looked at his legs. Long. Really, extraordinarily long. And unlike her own legs, she could see his muscle under the skin. She ran her hands down his thighs, feeling the dark, sparse hair and the bone of his knees.

"Shall I lift my hooves for you?" he asked. "Like I'm Zephyr?"

"Later," she said, smiling. "Would you turn around?"

He turned. A golden back. Narrow again but straight and strong so it did not look as vulnerable as it might have, otherwise. And his arse was…well, it was the most adorable thing. The cheeks were small and pert.

Maybe she had better never tell her husband his arse was adorable. Because *adorable* was for Nathaniel.

Arousing had to be the word for Oliver. His body was the body that had taken her flailing, young need and sharpened it to a point where he was the exemplar of male beauty. The nonesuch. He had made it so any tall, thin, masculine silhouette caused her heart to beat rapidly. But when it was his, her thighs would clench together and her nipples would harden.

He embodied her desire. He had embodied her desire as long as she had had desire.

"Are you finished now?" he said softly, still facing away, shifting his weight from one foot to the other so the cheeks of his bottom flexed.

"Not yet." She took her chemise up and over her head. "Now."

He pivoted. For a few seconds, his eyes were coolly appraising and then they turned a bit wild. One of his hands went to his cock and he stroked himself, seemingly unaware he was doing it in front of her.

"Oh, my God, you're so beautiful, and I want you so badly."

"Well then," she said, sliding away from the edge of the bed. "It's a good thing you're married to me."

He put one knee on the mattress. "You make me desperate for you."

"I like to see you desperate." She lay back and opened her arms. "But there's no need."

He came to her, pressing his whole body against hers, kissing her. As he clenched her hair in one hand and, with the other, touched her breasts, the soft folds of her belly, her thighs, he murmured nonsense between his kisses. Words like *goddess* and *decadent* and *you forever*.

He settled his hand between her legs.

"I know so little about pleasing you," he rasped. "Tell me."

"Put your finger in me…like it's your…cock," she said and hid her red face in his shoulder.

He slid his finger into her folds. "You're so wet here, Henrietta." His finger found her entrance, and his mouth descended on her nearest breast, and he began to suckle at her nipple again.

She clenched down immediately as his finger entered her. She was so hungry to be filled by him.

"Oh, yes," she moaned. "I'm ready."

"Not yet, Mrs. Hartwell." He added another finger. "How does that feel?" He moved the fingers in and out and suckled again at her breast.

"It feels…it feels like it should be your cock. Please, Oliver."

"Shall I take you from behind as I promised you?"

"I don't care…yes."

Before she knew what was happening, he was pulling her

away from the center of the mattress, propping her up on her knees so her back end faced the edge of the bed. And then he was off the bed and standing behind her, both of his hands on her hips, and she could feel his hard phallus in the crack between her cheeks and then sliding against the wetness of her inner lips.

"You're gorgeous from every angle, every position. All this beauty."

She loved hearing he thought her beautiful. She did. But she was frantic for him now. Wild to have him. She arched her spine and pushed back against him, needing him to enter her.

"So pretty. Too pretty."

"Oliver," she pleaded.

"My pretty wife. So very pretty even when you're begging for my cock."

She felt one hand come off her hip and some fumbling and the head of him stretched her entrance open.

She clenched. His hand came up and settled on the flat of her back, between her shoulder blades. "I want you, but I don't want to hurt you. You must relax and let me in. Can you do that for me, sweetheart?"

Sweetheart. The word sliced through the haze of her desire, made her own heart pound even faster than it was pounding already, filled her eyes with tears. Her forbidding, stern husband had just called her *sweetheart.*

Of course, all those roiling emotions made her want to tighten her muscles even more, hold his cock securely, never let him go, but his hand passed over her back in soothing strokes and she forced herself to relax her neck and dangle her head and soon her inner walls were also relaxing.

"So good, so beautiful, Henrietta."

She could feel him advancing, plunging in deeper now that she was not cinching her sex around his.

Oh, heavens. Her head snapped up. His cock had touched

some place deep inside her. Some place never touched before. Not last night. Not during her own explorations.

Some new paradise.

"Do that again," she said. "Please."

She felt him withdraw and plunge in again. Tingling ecstasy.

"Is that good?" he panted.

"It's…I'm…" She could not answer.

He did it again. And again. And then he leaned over her and she could feel the brush of his chest hair against her back and his hand clutched a breast and she knew his big hands had been meant for her big breasts.

The other hand came around her hip and went between her legs and when he touched her swollen bit and rubbed it, she exploded.

Spasms of pleasure in her belly and her core, a gush of fluid down her leg. Her head fell forward onto the bed as she screamed soundlessly, and she bit down on a fold in the sheet, and her fingers clutched at nothing.

She was barely aware Oliver was still thrusting into her, but from far away, she heard him say, "So beautiful, my beautiful wife, coming all over my cock."

And then he held himself deep inside her and groaned and jerked once, twice, thrice, and she felt his warmth and knew he had found his own release.

Eighteen

Seconds later, she was curled on her side in the bed and he was behind her, both of them still breathing heavily, their bodies dewed with perspiration.

When she found the wherewithal to speak, she said, "You called me *sweetheart*."

A silence stretched for several seconds. Then he said, "You are sweet. The sweetest person I know. And you are also my heart."

The blissful lethargy that had overtaken her after her release vanished in a sharp flare of feeling. It wasn't pain, but some cousin to it she had never felt before. She turned and faced him. She put her hand on his jaw and stared into his gray eyes. She had held herself back for so long, and she couldn't anymore.

"You are my heart, too. You've always been my heart."

He swallowed, his Adam's apple moving up and down. "I didn't know I had a heart until you."

"Yes, you did. But that's all right. I don't mind sharing."

Suddenly, the former Mrs. Hartwells couldn't hurt her now she knew the truth of her husband's desire for her. She had Oliver in her bed, and those other women couldn't take him away.

"Sharing?" His hands gripped her waist, and he pulled her to him with a roughness that thrilled her. "There's no sharing. You're mine. I'm yours."

She laughed. "I meant with Violet and Emily."

His face went still. And grim. "I should tell you about Violet and Emily."

"You don't have to." She ran a hand down his long flank. "Not if you don't want to."

"You deserve to know. What have you heard about my wives?"

He was so serious. Even for him. She felt a little frightened. "Nothing. Just what you've told me."

A few months ago, when he had shared a secret hurt from his past—losing his chance to roam the world and be an explorer—he had not looked at her. But now he gazed directly into her eyes, and even before he spoke, she saw his suffering.

"I met Violet at your parents' town house, at one of their dinner parties. I thought I was in love with her. But it was a foolish infatuation, nothing more. I didn't understand her. I didn't know her. I thought she was delightfully mercurial when she was actually dangerously volatile. And when I went to her father to ask for her hand, I didn't know she had no real interest in me or my courtship. She had only been using me as a pawn in a flirtation with another man."

"Oh, no."

"Her father forced her to accept my suit because of my land and money. Maybe because of my connection to your family. Only after we were married did I discover she loathed me."

"I'm sure she didn't, Oliver."

"Yes, she did." He looked away from Henrietta, but only for a second. "She told me so."

"Well, she was deranged, then."

Oliver put his hand against her face gently and ran his thumb over her lower lip. "Yes, she was. I know you didn't mean it in the literal sense, sweetheart, but she was. She was disturbed, deeply. And very unhappy. We lived separate lives in this house, for years. We had not— She didn't like me and she didn't like coupling with me. We barely spoke and when we did, it was mostly…well, she was cruel."

Anger sparked in Henrietta's heart. No one should have ever been cruel to Oliver. But she bit her tongue. She must let him talk. At long last, her husband was letting her in. She had asked to know his thoughts, and now he was telling her.

"One night, she came into my room while I was sleeping. I woke up with a knife to my throat."

Henrietta fumbled for Oliver's hands and gripped them tightly.

"I got away from her and the knife, but I didn't get the knife away from her. She used it to cut her own throat in front of me."

She could stay silent no longer. "She meant to hurt you. Oh, Oliver."

"I was not a good husband to her. It was my fault. I ignored her. I ignored her unhappiness."

What an agonizing burden her husband had carried. She was desperate to tell him how wrong he was, what a good husband he was to *her*, but she mustn't interrupt him, even though he was all wrong in his thinking.

"And then, years later, I wed Emily. Even now, I don't know how I had the strength to do so. She lived in the village and when her brother died and there was no other family, I married her to keep her out of the workhouse. I shouldn't have. I should have found another way. She reminded me so much of myself, very serious and quiet, and I was so full of self-hatred at that time. And I don't think she cared for me. She only felt a sense of obligation.

"And with her…Violet had not allowed me in her bed in years. I knew Emily's health was poor. I should have guessed she should not carry a child. But I went into her bed despite that. Because she let me. And I killed her."

Henrietta couldn't keep quiet. "You did not. Listen to me, Oliver Hartwell. You did not kill her. Women die in childbirth all the time."

He winced. "Don't say that."

"It's true."

"But I have been…I have been counting on the fact you're so strong that you…you won't die. I could not bear it. Nathaniel could not bear it. You mustn't die."

"We will do all we can to prevent it, won't we? But it's a risk I'm taking, gladly. I want a baby. I'm sure Emily wanted a baby."

"She did."

Henrietta got up on an elbow. "See? You married her and saved her from the workhouse which would have certainly killed her. You gave her a pregnancy she wanted. It's not your fault she didn't live to see and raise and love Nathaniel. And Violet? It sounds like she was so unhappy and in so much pain. I feel sorry for her. But I feel much more sorry for you because you have had to live with that horror."

No wonder Oliver had told her he would not impose on her. She finally understood why he had said such a thing.

She whispered, "You lived through some terrible times. But you're here with me now. With a woman who wants you very much. And wants your happiness."

"Yes." He covered his face with his hands. "Was I wrong to tell you?"

"No. No, no, no. I want you to share everything with me. Your sorrows and your joys."

He rubbed his eyelids with his fingertips and then took his hands away and gazed at her, blinking. "I can't help but be happy, married to you. You make me happy. I never thought I could be. And I never thought you could want me this way."

"I want to ask…it's silly, but…all this time…you wanted me?"

His angular face softened. "I wanted you ever since I saw you in the middle of your Season, in London. You were so beautiful and so hopeful and so alive. Everything I wasn't. And I hated myself for wanting you."

"Oh, Oliver."

"I've often wondered if I kissed you not just because I desired you more than any other woman in the world, but because I wanted to keep you for myself."

"I was already yours, foolish man. I used to wait for you, you know, to come out of my father's study."

He laughed.

Everything about tonight was a miracle. Her husband was in bed with her, *laughing*.

"Really? I always thought your mother had sent you in her place to make sure your father and I didn't stagger into anything after we had emptied the decanter."

"No, I just wanted to see you. And then I learned to make custard for you when I was sixteen."

"You learned for me?"

"Yes. But I didn't know you couldn't send custard from Bexton to Crossthwaite."

"No. You had to come to Crossthwaite and make it here."

"Yes." She sat up. "And now I'm a bit put out with myself. We wasted two years, Oliver."

He pulled her back down into the circle of his arms. "Don't be upset. Don't. I'm sorry you thought your husband didn't desire you, but it wasn't time wasted. When we married, I wasn't whole. Even if I had selfishly taken advantage of you, I would have been no kind of proper husband to you."

She nestled against him, wanting to get as close as possible to this glorious man who was finally hers in every way. "You needed time?"

He kissed her forehead. "I needed you. To show me the way. To teach me how to be a father to my son. To teach me how to appreciate life. And how to appreciate you."

"Two years, though."

"I promise you I went as quickly as I could. I had a lifetime of disappointment to unlearn. And the only reason I did it at all is because you're such a brilliant teacher. My bright, steady, unflinching star in the darkness."

She tilted her head and looked up at him. "And maybe, finally, because I asked you for a baby?"

"Yes. I had vowed to give you anything you asked for. I hadn't dared to dream you would ask for me."

"All right. I won't be upset I had to wait two years. It's my own fault for not asking sooner—" He tried to break in, but she spoke over him. "But you have to make me a promise."

"Anything."

"You'll compensate me now with lashings and lashings of baby-making."

"How much is lashings?"

"Every night?"

"Not the mornings, too?"

He was teasing her. Teasing from Oliver Hartwell was as intimate as having him inside her.

"The mornings, too. I'm very desirous of my husband, you see, and I need to be satisfied."

"Or?"

"Or nothing. I'm your wife, no matter what."

"I will do my best. But don't forget, you married an old man."

"I married an *older* man. Who has already given me my first son, the dearest boy in the whole world. Who has cared for me with a great deal of tenderness. But now…"

"Now?"

"Now, I'm ready for passion."

"I can't still care for you tenderly, Mrs. Hartwell?"

She reached up and stroked the lock over his forehead and wound it around her finger before tugging on it. "I will insist on it, Mr. Hartwell."

NINETEEN

It was the best night of not sleeping Oliver had ever had. They passed the hours talking and touching and kissing. At times, the kissing and touching took on an urgency and moved one or the other of them to climax—more often Henrietta than Oliver, since, after all, she was younger and he owed her all the pleasure she could demand from him. But, still, he was astonished by his own seemingly insatiable desire for her and her beauty.

The generosity of her loving spirit was matched in the generosity of her body. Her heavy, full breasts threatened to overflow his hands even as her oh-so sensitive dark-rose nipples hardened under his tongue. The heft of her tall, thick legs. Juicy, plump buttocks that made his mouth salivate. The velvety folds of skin and deep creases on her flanks. Her round belly curving down to her succulent quim.

And everything, everywhere, was all sweetly scented softness. All woman. His woman.

After he had found his fourth release of the night, she laughed. "You see? You're not an old man."

No, he wasn't. She made him young again. In fact, tonight he felt younger than he had ever felt in his actual youth.

Just before dawn, Henrietta sat up and wove her fingers through his.

"I want to show you something wonderful. Something I did. We must get out of bed and get dressed."

He obeyed her. He would always do anything she asked of him. Even though he thought they should never leave this bed and she should never again wear any clothes, existing always in a state of bare beauteousness.

He dressed and she put on her riding habit and he helped her, but he was so drunk on lust and affection, he did not think about what might happen next.

She took him out to the stables. One groom was already awake, checking on the horses.

"Will you get the saddle, Fenton? You know the one I mean." She winked.

"It's time to show your mister what you can do, eh?" The groom grinned.

It was a strange looking thing Fenton brought out from the harness room. Somewhat like a normal sidesaddle but with a horn sticking out the side and curved downwards.

He watched the groom and Henrietta put it on Zephyr.

"What's the extra horn for?"

She raised her eyebrows. "You'll see. Get your own horse saddled."

Henrietta was on Zephyr and waiting for him in the muddy stable-yard when he came out on his own mount. The sky had turned rosy with the dawn, as rosy as Henrietta's skin after she had experienced the heights of pleasure. He knew that now, and it gave him a proud and proprietary warmth in the middle of his chest.

"Follow me." His wife tilted her head in the direction of the sunrise and turned her horse and rode out.

She led him to one of the fields he owned. A pasture, empty of sheep right now but full of tall, ungrazed grasses, wet with last night's rain. There were rough stone walls along the edges and a hedgerow he had pleached himself running down the center. Henrietta turned Zephyr so she faced Oliver.

"My saddle is for jumping."

"Jumping?"

"When a rider is astride and he jumps his horse, he squeezes his legs together and keeps his seat because of that squeeze. But in a sidesaddle, there's no purchase for a good squeeze because the lady's legs don't go around the horse. You saw the extra horn? That's for my left leg. I squeeze the regular horn with my right leg and my left leg comes up and squeezes into the extra horn, and I can stay on Zephyr even during a jump. Do you want to see?"

"No." He had a horrible feeling.

"I've done it hundreds of times this summer. Oh, please, Oliver, I'm dying to show you."

"Is it safe?"

"There's nothing that's perfectly safe. You know that. We've talked about that."

Yes, they had. Henrietta was apt to let Nathaniel do all kinds of dangerous things. Climb trees, wade into meres. Oliver would prefer to wrap Nathaniel in cotton batting and never let the boy out of his sight now that he had finally admitted to himself how much he loved his son.

But part of love was encouraging someone's best qualities. Like bravery. Oliver didn't want his son to be fearful. He wanted him to have some mettle, like Henrietta and Crispin and all the Staffords did. He had been forcing himself, slowly and painfully, to let Nathaniel have some risk in his life. To let his son have courage while Oliver tried to find his own.

Zephyr snorted and stamped impatiently, but Henrietta

controlled him with the reins in one hand, patting his neck with the other.

"It's as safe as I could make it. And it's so exciting. Please let me show you."

She was his wife, and now he felt more protective of her bodily safety than ever. But he should not stifle her. He could not. He had vowed to give her what she wanted. She was a grown person of reason and sense, and she wanted this.

"Yes," he said. He got off his own horse and stood back.

Henrietta cantered Zephyr around the periphery of the field and then came galloping back towards Oliver and the hedgerow.

No. Stop. Turn back. He swallowed down his words and instead concentrated on his wife's fiercely exuberant face, her horse's indisputable strength and grace, how the two of them moved as one.

On the jump, Oliver held his breath, but Zephyr and Henrietta cleared the hedgerow easily. Together they were a creature in flight, soaring and exultant, capable of astounding feats.

He ran to vault the stone wall since he knew this was the fastest way around the hedgerow. As he did so, he heard screams.

His heart simultaneously choked him and sank into his belly.

But Henrietta was still on Zephyr, bringing the horse into a canter and a slower loop back around the field. She was screaming in triumph.

He ran to her through the wet, tall grasses as she rode towards him.

"Did you see that?" she shouted. "That's the highest we've ever taken, and for a moment, I didn't think—"

As she slowed Zephyr and Oliver came up beside them, he brought his arms up and gripped her waist. She didn't resist, taking her left foot out of its stirrup, putting her hands on his shoulders and sliding down.

"What's wrong? It went perfectly, didn't—"

He seized her face in his hands and turned it up and kissed her. Deeply. He poured everything he had into the contact of his lips on hers. His desire. His despair that she might have injured herself, been lost to him. His love.

Yes. Love. He loved this woman with every particle of his being. More than he would have ever thought possible. No one had ever loved someone as much he loved her.

His teeth clashed with hers, their breaths melded, and he groaned his love into her mouth.

When the kiss ended, she stared up at him, her lips apart, her blue eyes wide with astonishment.

"You," he panted. "You are the most impossibly beautiful and wonderful woman I have ever known. And I've done everything wrong with you. I ignored you and then I ruined you and then I wed you and then I loved you and then I tried to give you a baby and then…I'm sorry."

"Say that again," she breathed.

"I'm sorry."

"No." She swallowed. "The part where you said you loved me."

"Love." He grabbed a fistful of her hair. "There is no love here without you. I don't have a son without you, do you understand? Do you think Nathaniel would love his father if you hadn't taught him about love? If you hadn't taught both of us?"

"You love me," she whispered and touched his cheek. Her fingertips glistened when she brought her hand away.

He was crying, he realized.

"Yes, yes, yes. I love you." He lifted his head toward the sky and shouted, "I love Henrietta Hartwell!"

She laughed. "And I love Oliver Hartwell."

He brought his eyes to hers. "You do?"

"So much."

"You…" he faltered. "You're so important. More than important. It's not enough…I have to tell you. I was wrong. You see, I thought you were my lodestar."

She tilted her head. "Lodestar?"

"A lodestar is…it's a heavenly body used for navigation. And I thought you were the thing by which I would steer the rest of my life. But I was wrong. You're not."

"I'm not?"

"No. You're all the stars, Henrietta. You're the sky, the sun, the moon, the ocean, the boat, the whole damn thing. You're everything. Everything."

In the pink-golden dawn, the kiss his wife gave back to him was everything, too.

It was her lust, her love, her life. It was her joy.

It was Henrietta, his everything.

First Epilogue
January. 1820.

A knock on the bedchamber door made Henrietta break away from kissing Oliver despite his protests, his hands trailing over her body as she rose from the bed. The bedchamber was quite warm because Oliver had built up the fire in preparation for their intimacy, but for modesty's sake, Henrietta tied a dressing gown over her chemise before opening the door to the hallway. A tearful Nathaniel stood there, shivering.

"What's wrong, darling? Did you have a bad dream?" She leaned over and picked him up. He had gotten so much taller and heavier, but she was glad he still let her hold him this way.

"Yes. Can I sleep with you?" Nathaniel must have seen Oliver in her bed over her shoulder. "Did Papa have a bad dream, too?"

She half-laughed. "Something like that." She turned and walked back to the bed, carrying Nathaniel. She didn't know how Oliver would feel about the interruption, so she made a funny face at him over Nathaniel's head.

Oh, no. Oliver had managed to pull his shirt back on, but he was frowning and looked so severe.

Still, she slid Nathaniel into the bed next to his father and followed the boy quickly under the warm covers.

Oliver laid his large hand on Nathaniel's chest. "What was this bad dream about? Do I need to go thrash some dragons up in the nursery?"

Of course, Oliver's frown had been for the bad dream, not for Nathaniel coming into her bed for comfort. She was always a molten puddle of adoration for her husband, but, if possible, she melted a little more.

"No," Nathaniel said seriously. "My bad dreams don't have dragons."

Oliver propped himself up on an elbow. "What do they have?"

Nathaniel cast a sly glance at Henrietta and then rolled towards his father and put his mouth to Oliver's ear and whispered.

"Yes," Oliver said when Nathaniel was done. "That is a very bad dream. But it's not going to happen, all right?"

Nathaniel lay back. "All right."

"Maybe Nathaniel better stay here until he falls asleep," Henrietta said to Oliver, still a trifle anxious about what her amorous husband might think of that idea.

"An excellent notion." Oliver lay back himself, his head next to Nathaniel's on the pillow. "As long as you tell us both the caterpillar story."

So, for what seemed, and might actually be, the thousandth time, Henrietta began the story of the caterpillar who liked to crawl and creep and climb.

It didn't take long for both of the Hartwell men's eyes to close, for Nathaniel's face to go slack. Henrietta reached out and stroked the shining curl in the middle of her husband's forehead.

"He's asleep," she whispered.

"So am I," Oliver whispered back. But his actions belied

his words. He opened his eyes and in the quick, graceful way he had, he scooped Nathaniel up in his arms and padded across the room.

He turned at the door. "I expect you to be unclothed by the time I return," he growled.

Henrietta shed her dressing gown and chemise as soon as the door closed, wriggling into the warmth of the bed with anticipatory delight.

She *loved* when Oliver growled at her.

In only a few minutes, Oliver was back in her bedchamber, stripping off his shirt.

"I missed you," she said with a pretend-pout as Oliver climbed into the bed, under the covers, but over her.

He kissed the base of her throat. "I'm sorry I was occupied by escorting our young chaperone back to his own bed."

She threw her arms around his neck, and he lowered his full weight onto her. What a pleasure it was to have his body against hers. His smooth skin. His spare, hard form. She let her hands run over his shoulders and his sharp shoulder blades. Her husband.

"I hope you were not too jealous about another male in my bed," she teased.

He pulled his head back and assessed her with his gray eyes.

"No. Not Nathaniel. If there's one thing I know, it's that Mrs. Hartwell has enough love for both of us. We will never go wanting for that."

"That's true. And maybe there's enough love for more?"

He was off of her and onto the mattress at her side before she could clutch at him and keep him on top of her.

"More? As in more children?"

Without thought, her hand went to her lower belly. "One more, at least."

His hand joined hers, cupping her soft roundness. "And you are well?"

"Very well," she assured him. "So far."

"So far? How far is that?"

"Oh," she temporized. "Not so very far." He waited. "Two or three months, I think."

His eyebrows went down into a deep *V*. "Two or three months? Why did you keep it from me for so long?"

"I was not sure…it had really taken. And, of course, I wanted to be sure you would continue to come to my bed once I was with child."

"Just try to keep me out of your bed." He took her mouth with a fierceness that made her shiver.

Then his face softened, his eyes became worried, so like Nathaniel's with his bad dream. "Unless it is not good for you or the child?"

She cupped his jaw, dark and rough with evening whiskers, and her fingertips brushed the fine lines radiating from his eye to his temple. "It's very good for me. And long ago, my mother assured me acts of love do not harm an unborn baby."

He turned his face into her hand and kissed her palm before speaking. "Can I get you to agree to no hedgerow jumping until the baby comes?"

"Yes. As it turns out, I am not as fond of jumping as I thought I would be. I haven't done any since I first missed my courses."

"But I thought…all your work on the saddle?"

"I wanted to make something for myself. And I did."

He brushed a curl of hair off her cheek. "I'm glad you made something for yourself."

"And now I'm making something for both of us. And for Nathaniel."

"I am even more glad of that."

He rolled on top of her again and his kiss was tender and

lingering as he held her face between his hands and consumed her mouth with a slow heat. She answered his caressing tongue with a whimper as he pushed her deep into the mattress, his hard cock against her leg, making his desire known to her in no uncertain terms.

"God, you're so lovely," he breathed as he moved down, stippling her throat with soft kisses. "Every square inch of you." He nipped at the delicate bit of flesh where her neck ended and her shoulder began. "I want to eat you like you're custard."

His hands were on the sides of her breasts, holding them, squeezing them. He slid farther down her body and gathered her breasts together. One thumb went over a peak, hardening it. Then his mouth descended and he sucked lightly, causing exquisite ripples of pleasure to spread from her breast to her already aching core.

She could not stop herself from arching against him, desperate for more, feverishly pushing her nipple at his mouth.

But he lifted his head, pulled his mouth away, seared her with the heat in his gaze. "You like that, Henrietta? You like me holding your teats, kissing and suckling them? You like knowing these beautiful breasts drive me mad with desire? Make me hard as a rock when I see them or touch them or even think about them?"

"I…like…" Her speech was leaving her as it so often did when her passion was whipped into a frenzy by her husband's touch.

"I know what you like." His large hands curved around her breasts, exerting a bit more pressure, the squeezing coming closer to a kneading. "I know what you like, my irresistible, irrepressible, wanton wife."

He put his head down, his nose skimming over the skin in the valley where her breasts met as he pushed them together. He inhaled deeply and kissed her there. "So sweet."

"Oliver," she bleated, wild now for something more, raising her hips, searching, wanting, needing.

He gripped her thighs forcefully together with his own legs and pushed her pelvis back down as he took the other breast into his mouth and began to suck.

Her hands sunk into his silky, raven hair and he responded by worrying at her nipple with a bit more ferocity, grazing it with his teeth and sucking at it sharply.

"Oliver. I need…you."

He looked up at her but did not stop his attentions to her breast, raising his eyebrows slightly.

She bucked. "Need."

Finally, he released her nipple. "I need, too, Henrietta. I need a taste of you, of your sweetness down below. I need to pleasure you with my tongue."

He was moving even farther down, his hands still clamped possessively on her breasts, but now his chin was just above her thatch of copper curls and she was moving her knees apart, driven by her hunger to have him between her legs. His cock, his hand, his face, his tongue, his anything.

Settling himself onto the mattress, he released her breasts and brought his arms down and spread her legs even wider.

"I need to see all this beauty you hide here."

Her entire cleft already felt so swollen and aching and throbbing, desperate for his touch.

"Please," she whispered as his hands reverently ran over her abundant hips and he kissed the tender curves at the tops of thighs, right next to her sex. "Please."

"As you wish."

Yes, he was so good to her and always did what she asked. Except in cases when he knew her ecstasy would be even more heightened by a prolonged, sensual exploration than the rush to climax she begged for. Not that Oliver himself wasn't prone to a certain furious and wicked hunger, coming upon her in the middle of the day and throwing up her skirts and thrilling her with a quick, savage coupling in some unlikely place like, say, the harness room.

He blew a stream of air over her spread, vulnerable self. She knew his breath was warm, but against her wet folds, it felt wonderfully cool. But his breath was not his touch. She needed his touch. Would he continue to tease her or would he satisfy her?

Tease, she decided. Because of how he had played with her breasts.

But she was wrong. He did not dally but immediately began to worship her bit, providing firm but gentle pressure with his mouth as his stubble scraped deliciously against her skin.

It was just as she liked, just as she wanted.

"Oh," she sighed and abandoned herself to the churn of pleasure as her fingers sifted through his ebony locks. "Yes." She loved his tongue and his lips and all the sensations he gave her with them.

But she was greedy and as her arousal grew, she strained against his strong hands holding her hips down, pinning her to the mattress. She bucked her pelvis up, wanting more, even more, her need intense and overwhelming. Oliver slapped the side of her hip, a reminder he was in control, and she quieted and tried to hold herself still, but she could not for long.

After another buck, he raised his head.

"Are you determined to ride my face, my valkyrie?"

"Oh, Oliver, please, I want to…please, let me ride your cock."

She loved to have him inside her while she was atop him. And she thought he loved it, too.

He gave her one of his rare smiles, and in seconds, he was flat on his back on the mattress and she was astride his narrow hips. She stroked each one of his hip bones with her thumbs and then eased herself down over his hard cock.

Yes.

This joining, this fullness was so right. It was more than pleasure. It was more than creating a child. It was union.

His long arms reached out and his hands ran over her thighs, her hips, the folds at her waist, and settled on her breasts.

She ground herself against him, using the bone at the base of his cock against her nub. He watched her, his mouth open, his gray eyes darkening, and he pulled at her nipples, pinching them.

She moved more quickly, up and down on his shaft, using her strong thighs to power their shared pleasure.

"Henrietta, I…I…"

He didn't need to tell her. She knew he was close. She leaned forward and kissed his mouth and then resumed riding him at a fast and vigorous pace, her torso above him, just like he was her mount.

Her husband mount.

"Come for me, Oliver."

"But you haven't…"

"I will."

His face smoothed, his eyes closed, and his hips thrust up. As she felt his hot release, she touched her nub and brought herself to a climax that took all her strength in long, sensuous waves of abandon and collapsed her down against him. She shuddered in ecstasy as the pleasure pulsed through her body and he held her in his arms and kissed her hair and said, "So beautiful, my love."

They lay there for a long time, sated, drowsing.

Only one thing kept Henrietta from sleep. From her position on top of Oliver, she asked, "What did Nathaniel say his bad dream was about? The thing you promised wouldn't happen?"

Oliver tightened his clasp around her. "He said he dreamed Mama went away and left us alone."

But that *had* happened. Nathaniel's mother had left him, against her will and likely in agony, knowing her son would never remember his mother.

Oliver whispered, "He meant you."

She pulled away and looked into his eyes. "Me?"

"You're his mother, Henrietta. You've been his mother for a long time now. And I've been a fool, not wanting you to feel an obligation. Not wanting you chained to us, when you deserved to be free."

She brushed his lips with hers. "I want the obligation. I choose the obligation. That is freedom."

"Will you let Nathaniel call you Mama?"

"Let?" She laughed and hugged Oliver and wriggled in joy. "He must. After all, we don't want his sister to call me a different name than he does."

Oliver raised his eyebrows. "Sister?"

"I'm sure he would want a brother, so if we prepare him for a sister, he won't be disappointed."

"I'm not so sure he would want a brother. He's very wise, you know. He may look ahead and realize a sister almost six years younger than he is will have many pretty friends of a marriageable age when he starts looking for a wife."

She snorted in laughter but then had to ask, "What do you want, Oliver?"

He stroked her hair. "You."

"No, silly. In a baby."

"I want whatever you'll give me. I just hope the little thing won't hurt you too much."

"I'm not delicate."

"No, you're not." He cradled her hips in his hands.

"That's what I'm depending on. That, and the vow I took. Or rather, the bargain I made with God."

"What bargain?"

"That I would give or do anything you asked of me, and in return, you would not leave."

She pretended indignation. "You should have made the bargain with me."

"Oh, but you might have asked for all kinds of expensive fripperies such as new drawing room curtains."

"I would not have!"

"No, you wouldn't. Just saddle-making lessons. A stable for your horse. A baby. And my and Nathaniel's hearts."

"I never asked for your hearts. Those had to be given."

"You have them all the same."

"Good. Because I want them. And I'm never giving them back."

He raised his eyebrows. "You might have to give Nathaniel's back in a score of years, or so."

She dismissed that far-off complication with a laugh and a kiss to Oliver's chin. "Oh, that's the future. Let's stay here. And now. Just us three."

"Just us three. And one-third."

She didn't understand at first, but his large hands gently squeezed her around her waist and then she did.

More About
Voluptuous
and Oliver & Henrietta and Crispin & Georgiana and The Bed Me Books

Voluptuous is a complete story, but I always like to have a little more time in the happily-ever-after. So, I wrote a second epilogue to give myself (and my readers) a bit more Henrietta and Oliver. To get the free second epilogue, please subscribe to my newsletter at www.felicityniven.com/voluptuous (even if you are already subscribed, you have to sign up again at that webpage).

I like to think of my second epilogues as an extra dollop of custard for being in the loyalty club (i.e., a newsletter subscriber).

Also, at the time of printing, there is a prequel short story to ***Voluptuous*** entitled ***Be Not Coy***, available for sale on Amazon. It features the instalust and meet-cute story of Henrietta's parents, Crispin and Georgiana. And you get a glimpse of a nineteen-year-old Oliver.

And Henrietta and Oliver and Nathaniel will also appear in ***Bed Me, Viscount***. This full-length novel takes place at Crossthwaite and is what happens when "just us three" is disrupted by unplanned visits from Henrietta's sister Ellen and Oliver's cousin William Dagenham.

At this time, **Voluptuous** is part of **The Bed Me Books** series. In terms of reading order, **Voluptuous** should come directly before **Bed Me, Viscount** and serve as a prequel to that book. And, yes, **Be Not Coy** is a short story prequel to **Voluptuous** so it's a pre-prequel to **Bed Me, Viscount**.

I tend to weave a tangled web. Forgive me.

Author's Notes

Oliver and Henrietta marry by common license which does not require banns to be read. The couple must have permission from a bishop, marry within the church of either the bride or groom's parish, and pay a fee. Henrietta also needs her parents' consent because she is not yet twenty-one.

In the time period of this story, the type of vehicle known as a *brake* would have most likely been spelled *break*. However, to avoid confusion, I have deliberately used the more modern spelling *brake*.

The two-pommel (or "leaping horn") sidesaddle that makes jumping far safer for sidesaddle riders was actually thought to have been first devised in the 1830s by French riding-master Jules Pellier.

Acknowledgments

I am always grateful to anyone who reads anything I've ever written. Readers make my world spin, get me to turn on my laptop, keep me dreaming.

Thank you to my friends who read this book before it was complete: Alexandra Gall, Shannon Lawson, Melinda Greathouse, Kat Sterling, Jane Maguire. And thank you to Bree who performed a sensitivity read. I appreciate all the feedback I received. It was invaluable. However, all errors or missteps are mine and mine alone.

I have to thank Molly Gunn who has more courage than anyone else. Thank you to Jace Anderson who made me aspire to be an artist again. Thank you to Julia Quinn for the encouragement. Thank you to Alexandra Gall who has become a true friend through the internet. And thank you to Alexandra Vasti who is invariably so generous and so kind while simultaneously being so brilliant (how does she do that?).

And thank you to my wonderful and beautiful mother who introduced me to historical romance.

About the Author

Felicity Niven is a hopeful romantic. Writing Regency romance is her third career after two degrees from Harvard. And you know what they say about third things? Yep, it's a charm. She splits her time between the temperate South in the winter and the cool Great Lakes in the summer and thinks there can be no greater comforts than a pot of soup on the stove, a set of clean sheets on the bed, and a Jimmy Stewart film on a screen in the living room. She is the author of ***The Bed Me Books*** series and ***The Lovelocks of London*** series.

Subscribers to Felicity's newsletter receive free second epilogues, prequel novellas, and holiday stories. Go to www.felicityniven.com/voluptuous and sign up now for the newsletter in order to receive the free second epilogue to ***Voluptuous***. Readers can follow Felicity on social media and join *The Ungovernables* on Facebook, a historical romance book club where Felicity co-hosts a monthly discussion of notable works in the historical romance canon.